"I don't usually do this," he said.

He didn't usually kidnap women or unbutton their wedding gowns?

Crista knew she should ask. No, she shouldn't ask. She should move now, back away, lock herself in the bathroom until her emotions were under control.

But he slowly lifted his hand. His fingertips grazed her shoulder. Then his palm cradled her neck, slipping up to her hairline. The touch was smooth and warm, his obvious strength couched by tenderness.

She couldn't bring herself to pull away. In fact, it was a fight to keep from leaning into his caress.

Jackson dipped his head.

She knew what came next. Anybody would know what came next.

His lips touched hers, kissing her gently, testing her texture and then her taste. Arousal instantly flooded her body. He stepped forward, his free arm going around her waist, settling at the small of her back, strong and hot against her exposed skin.

She didn't move away.

* * *

His Stolen Bride is part of the Chicago Sons series: Men who work hard, love harder and live with their fathers' legacies...

Dear Reader,

Welcome to book four of the Chicago Sons series! I love a great wedding, and when I was in my twenties I attended a lot of them. As you might imagine, they covered the spectrum from a picnic service in the park to a cathedral ceremony and a country club reception.

As the years went on, with certain exceptions, I began to notice a pattern: the bigger the wedding, the higher the probability of an eventual divorce. I wondered over the years if it might be due to a focus on the wedding versus a focus on the marriage. I'm still not sure, but it seemed like a fine starting point for a story.

Investigator Jackson Rush puts a sudden stop to Crista Corday's opulent wedding. He has his reasons for kidnapping her and holding her, designer gown and all, on his boat in Lake Michigan. Crista is determined to escape from the sexy, intimidating Jackson. But instead she kisses him and takes comfort from him, and finds herself questioning her own life choices.

Happy reading. I hope you enjoy *His Stolen Bride*!

Barbara

BARBARA DUNLOP

———

HIS STOLEN BRIDE

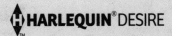
HARLEQUIN® DESIRE

Recycling programs
for this product may
not exist in your area

ISBN-13: 978-0-373-73472-6

His Stolen Bride

Printed in U.S.A.

www.Harlequin.com

A12006 831987

Barbara Dunlop writes romantic stories while curled up in a log cabin in Canada's far north, where bears outnumber people and it snows six months of the year. Fortunately she has a brawny husband and two teenage children to haul firewood and clear the driveway while she sips cocoa and muses about her upcoming chapters. Barbara loves to hear from readers. You can contact her through her website, barbaradunlop.com.

Books by Barbara Dunlop

Harlequin Desire

Visit the Author Profile page at Harlequin.com, or barbaradunlop.com, for more titles.

To Mom with love

One

A heavy metal door clanged shut behind Jackson Rush, echoing down the hallway of the Riverway State Correctional Institute in northeast Illinois. He paused to mentally brace himself as he took in the unfamiliar surroundings. Then he walked forward, his boot heels clacking against the worn linoleum. He couldn't help thinking the prison would make a perfect movie set, with its cell bars, scarred gray cinder blocks, flickering fluorescent lights and the scattered shouts from connecting rooms and hallways.

His father, Colin Rush, had been locked up here for nearly seventeen years, ever since he was caught stealing thirty-five million dollars from the unsuspecting investors in his personal Ponzi scheme.

His dramatic arrest had taken place on Jackson's thirteenth birthday. The police rushed the backyard pool party, sending guests shrieking and scattering. Jackson could still see the two-tiered blue-and-white layer cake sliding from the table, splattering on the grass, obliterating his name as it oozed into a pile of goo.

At first, his father had stridently proclaimed his innocence. Jackson's mother had taken Jackson to the courtroom every day of the trial, where they'd sat stoically and supportively behind the defense. But it soon became clear that Colin was guilty. Far from being a brilliant investor, he was a common thief.

When one of his former clients committed suicide, he lost all public sympathy and was sentenced to twenty years in jail. Jackson hadn't seen his father since.

Now he rounded the corner to the visiting area, prepared for stark wooden benches, Plexiglas partitions and hardwired black telephone receivers. Instead, he was surprised to find himself in a bright, open room that looked like a high school cafeteria. A dozen round red tables were positioned throughout, each with four stools connected by thick metal braces directly to the table base. The hall had high rectangular windows and checkerboard tile floors. A few guards milled around while the other visitors seemed to be mostly families.

A man stood up at one of the tables and made eye contact. It took Jackson a moment to recognize his father. Colin had aged considerably, showing deep wrinkles around his eyes and along his pale, hollow cheeks. His posture was stooped, and his hairline had receded. But there was no mistaking it was him, and he smiled.

Jackson didn't smile back. He was here under protest. He didn't know why his father had insisted he come, only that the emails and voice messages had become increasingly frequent and sounded more and more urgent. He'd eventually relented in order to make them stop.

Now he marched toward the table, determined to get the visit over and done with.

"Dad," he greeted flatly, sticking out his hand, pre-empting what would surely be the most awkward hug in history.

"Hello, son," said Colin, emotion shimmering in his eyes as he shook Jackson's hand.

His grip was firmer than Jackson had expected.

Jackson's attention shifted to a second man seated at the round table, half annoyed by his presence, but half curious as well.

"It's good to see you," said Colin.

Jackson didn't respond, instead raising his brow inquiringly at the stranger.

Colin cleared his throat and released Jackson's hand. "Jackson, this is Trent Corday. Trent and I have been cell mates for the past year."

It seemed more than strange that Colin would bring a friend to this meeting. But Jackson wasn't about to waste time dwelling on the question.

He looked back to his father. "What is it you want?"

He could only guess there must be a parole hearing coming up. If there was, Colin was on his own. Jackson wouldn't help him get out of prison early. Colin had three years left on his sentence, and as far as Jackson was concerned, he deserved every minute.

His selfish actions had harmed dozens of victims, not the least of which was Jackson's mother. She'd been inconsolable after the trial, drinking too much, abusing prescription painkillers, succumbing to cancer five years later just as Jackson graduated from high school.

Colin gestured to one of the stools. "Please, sit."

Jackson perched himself on the small metal seat.

"Trent has a problem," said Colin, sitting down himself.

What Trent's problem could possibly have to do with Jackson was the first question that came to mind. But he didn't ask—instead, he waited.

Trent filled the silence. "It's my daughter. I've only been inside for three years. A misunderstanding, really, I—"

"Save it," said Jackson.

Seventeen years ago, he'd listened to Colin protest endlessly about how he'd been framed, then railroaded, then misunderstood. Jackson wasn't here to listen to the lies of a stranger.

"Yes, well…" Trent glanced away.

Jackson looked at his watch.

"She's fallen victim," said Trent. He fished into the pocket of his blue cotton shirt. "It's the Gerhard family. I don't know if you've heard of them."

Jackson gave a curt nod.

Trent put a photograph on the table in front of Jackson. "Isn't she beautiful?"

Jackson's gaze flicked down.

The woman in the picture was indeed beautiful, likely in her midtwenties, with rich auburn hair, a bright, open smile, shining green eyes. But her looks were a moot point.

"She's getting married," said Trent. "To Vern Gerhard. They hide it well. But that family's known to a lot of the guys in here. Vern is a con artist and a crook. So is his father, and his father before that."

The woman obviously had questionable taste in men. Jackson found that less than noteworthy. In his line of work, he'd come across plenty of women who'd married the wrong guy, even more whose husbands didn't meet with the approval of their fathers. Again, this had nothing to do with him.

He looked back to Colin. "What is it *you* want from me?"

"We want you to stop the wedding," said Colin.

It took a second for the words to compute inside Jackson's head. "Why would I do anything like that?"

"He's after her money," said Trent.

"She's a grown woman." Jackson's glance strayed to the photo again.

She looked to be twenty-six or twenty-seven. He doubted she was thirty. With a face like that and any kind of money in the mix, she had to know she was going to attract a few losers. If she didn't recognize them herself, there wasn't anything Jackson could do about it.

Colin spoke up again. "She can't possibly know she's being conned. The girl places a huge value on honesty and integrity, has done her entire life. If she knew the truth, she wouldn't have anything to do with him."

"So tell her."

"She won't speak to me," said Trent. "She sure won't listen to me. She doesn't trust me as far as she can throw me."

"I'm sure you can relate to that particular viewpoint," said Colin, an edge to his voice.

"*That's* what you want to say to me?" Jackson rose to his feet. No way, no how was he buying into a guilt trip from his old man.

"Sit down," said Colin.

"Please," said Trent. "Year ago, I put something in her name, shares in a diamond mine."

"Lucky for her."

The woman might well be picking the wrong husband, but at least she'd have a comfortable lifestyle.

"She doesn't know about it," said Trent.

For the first time since he'd walked in, Jackson's curiosity was piqued. "She doesn't know she owns a diamond mine?"

Both men shook their heads.

Jackson looked at the picture again, picking it up from the table. She didn't appear naive. In fact, if he had to guess, he'd say she looked intelligent. But she was drop-dead gorgeous. In his eight years as a private detective, he'd discovered features like that made women targets.

"Hear us out," said Colin. "Please, son."

"Don't call me that."

"Okay. Fine. Whatever you want." Colin was nodding again.

"You hear things in here. And the Gerhards are dangerous," said Trent.

"More dangerous than you two felons?" Jackson didn't like that he'd become intrigued by the circumstances, but he had.

"Yes," said Trent.

Jackson hesitated for a beat, but then he sat back down. Another ten minutes wouldn't kill him.

"They found out about the mine," said Trent, his tone earnest.

"You know this for sure?" asked Jackson.

"I do."

"How?"

"A friend of a friend. The Borezone Mine made a promising new discovery a year ago. Only days later, Vern Gerhard made contact with my daughter. Final assaying is about to be announced, and the value will go through the roof."

"Is it publicly traded?" asked Jackson.

"Privately held."

"Then how did Gerhard know about the discovery?"

"Friends, industry contacts, rumors. It's not that hard if you know where to ask."

"It could be a coincidence."

"It's not." There was cold anger in Trent's voice. "The Gerhards are bottom-feeders. They heard about the discovery. They targeted her. And as soon as the ink is dry on the marriage certificate, they'll rob her blind and dump her like last week's trash."

Jackson traced his index finger around the woman's face. "You have proof of that? You have evidence that he's not in love with her?"

With that fresh-faced smile and those intelligent eyes, Jackson could imagine any number of men could simply fall in love, money or no money.

"That's what we need you for," said Colin.

"Expose their con," said Trent. "Look into their secret, slimy business dealings and tell my Crista what you find. Convince her she's being played and stop that wedding."

Crista. Her name was Crista. It suited her.

Despite himself, Jackson was beginning to think his way through the problem, calculate the time he'd need for a cursory look into the Gerhard family's business. At the moment, things weren't too busy in the Chicago office of Rush Investigations. He'd planned to use the lull to visit the Boston office and discuss a possible expansion. But if push came to shove, he could make some time for this.

She was pretty. He'd give her that. Nobody in the Boston office was anywhere near this pretty.

"Will you do it?" asked Colin.

"I'll scratch the surface," said Jackson, pocketing the photo.

Trent opened his mouth, looking like he might protest Jackson taking the picture. But he obviously thought better of it and closed his mouth again.

"Keep us posted?" asked Colin.

For a split second, Jackson wondered if this was all a ruse to keep him in contact with his father. Did Colin plan to string him along for a while for some hidden reason of his own? He was, after all, a gifted con artist.

"The wedding's Saturday," said Trent.

That diverted Jackson's attention. "*This* Saturday?"

"Yes."

That was three days away.

"Why didn't you start this sooner?" Jackson demanded. What did they expect him to accomplish in only three days?

"We did," Colin said quietly.

Jackson clamped his jaw. Yeah, his father had been trying to get hold of him for a month. He'd been studiously ignoring the requests, just like he'd been doing for years. He owed Colin nothing.

He stood. "It's not much time, but I'll see what I can find."

"She *cannot* marry him." Trent's undertone was rock hard with vehemence.

"She's a grown woman," Jackson repeated.

He'd look into the Gerhards. But if Crista Corday had fallen for a bad boy, there might be nothing her daddy or anyone else could do to change her mind.

* * *

Crista Corday swayed back and forth in front of the full-length mirror, her strapless lace and tulle wedding gown rustling softly against her legs. Her hair was swept up in a profusion of curls and braids. Her makeup had been meticulously applied. Even her underwear was white silk perfection.

She stifled a laugh at the absurdity of it all. She was a struggling jewelry designer, living in a basement suite off Winter Street. She didn't wear antique diamonds. She didn't get married in the magnificent Saint Luke's Cathedral with a reception at the Brookbend Country Club. And she didn't get swept off her feet by the most eligible prince charming in all of greater Chicago.

Except for the part where she did, and she had.

Cinderella had nothing on her.

There was a knock on the Gerhard mansion's bedroom door.

"Crista?" the male voice called out. It was Vern's cousin Hadley, one of the groomsmen.

"Come in," she called in return.

She liked Hadley. He was a few years younger than Vern, laid-back by Gerhard standards, fun-loving and friendly. Taller than most of the men in the family, he was athletic and good-looking, with a jaunty swath of dark blond hair that swooped across his forehead.

He lived in Boston rather than Chicago, but he visited often, sometimes staying at the mansion, sometimes using a hotel. Crista assumed he preferred a hotel when he had a date. Vern's mother, Delores, was staunchly religious and would not have allowed Hadley to have an overnight guest.

The door opened, and he stepped into the spacious,

sumptuously decorated guest room. Crista had spent the night here, while Vern had stayed in his apartment downtown. Maybe it was Dolores's influence, but Crista had been feeling old-fashioned the past few weeks, insisting she and Vern sleep apart until the honeymoon. Vern had reluctantly agreed.

Hadley halted. Then he pushed the door shut behind him and seemed to take in her ensemble.

"What?" she asked, checking herself out, wondering if she'd missed some glaring flaw.

"You look amazing," he said.

Crista scoffed. "I sure hope I do." She spread her arms. "Do you have any idea how much this all cost?"

Hadley grinned. "Aunt Delores wouldn't have it any other way."

"I feel like an impostor." Crista's stomach fluttered with a resurgence of apprehension.

"Why?" he asked. His tone was gentle, and he moved closer.

"Because I grew up on the lower west side."

"You don't think we're your people?"

She turned back to the mirror and gazed at her reflection. The woman staring back was her, but not her. It was a surreal sensation.

"Do you think you're my people?" she asked him.

"If you want us to be," he said.

Their gazes met in the mirror.

"But it's not too late," he added.

"Too late for what?"

"To back out." He looked serious, but he had to be joking.

"You're wrong about that." Not that she wanted to back out. Not that she'd even consider backing out. In fact, she couldn't imagine how their conversation had come to this.

"You look scared," he said.

"Of the wedding, sure. I'm probably going to trip on my way down the aisle. But I'm not afraid of the marriage."

It was Vern. She was marrying smart, respectful, polite Vern. The man who'd stepped up to invest in her jewelry design company, who'd introduced her to the finer things, who'd swept her away for a fantasy weekend in New York City and another in Paris. There wasn't much about Vern that wasn't fantastic.

"The future in-laws?" Hadley asked.

Crista quirked a smile. "Intimidated, not afraid."

The intensity left his expression, and he smiled in return. "Who wouldn't be intimidated by them?"

"Nobody I know, that's for sure."

Manfred Gerhard was a humorless workaholic. He was exacting and demanding, with a cutting voice and an abrupt manner. His wife, Delores, was prim and uptight, excruciatingly conscious of the social hierarchy, but skittish whenever Manfred was in the room, constantly catering to his whims.

If Vern ever acted like his father, Crista would kick him to the curb. No way, no how would she put up with that. Then the thought brought her up short. Vern wasn't at all like his father. She'd never seen anything to even suggest he might behave like Manfred.

"He's very close to them," said Hadley.

He was watching her intently again, and for a split second Crista wondered if he could read her thoughts.

"He's talking about buying an apartment in New York City." She liked the idea of putting some distance between Vern and his family. He loved them dearly, but she couldn't see spending every Sunday evening at the mansion the way Vern seemed to like.

"I'll believe that when it happens," said Hadley.

But Crista knew it was already decided. "It's so I can expand the business," she elaborated.

"Are you having second thoughts?" asked Hadley.

"No." She turned to face him. She wasn't. "What makes you say that? What makes you ask that?"

"Maybe I want you for myself."

"Very funny."

He hesitated for a moment then gave an unconcerned shrug. "I'm not sure I'd marry into this family."

"Too bad you're already in this family."

He looked her straight in the eyes. "So, you're sure?"

"I'm sure. I love him, Hadley. And he loves me. Everything else will work itself out around that."

He gave a nod of acquiescence. "Okay. If I can't get you to call off the wedding, then I'm here to tell you the limos have arrived."

"It's time?" The flutter in her stomach turned into a spasm.

It was perfectly normal, she told herself. She was about to walk down the aisle in front of hundreds of people, including her future in-laws and a who's who list of notable Chicagoans. She'd be a fool to be calm under these circumstances.

"You just turned pale," said Hadley.

"I told you, I'm afraid of tripping halfway down the aisle."

"You want me to walk you?"

"That's not how we rehearsed it."

Crista's father was in prison, and she didn't have a close male relative to escort her down the aisle. And in this day and age, it seemed ridiculous to scramble for a figurehead to "give her away" to Vern. She was walking down the aisle alone, and she was perfectly fine with that.

"I could still do it," said Hadley.

"No, you can't. You need to stand up front with Vern. Otherwise the numbers will be off, more bridesmaids than groomsmen. Dolores would faint dead away."

Hadley straightened the sleeves of his tux. "You got that right."

Crista pictured her six bridesmaids at the front of the cathedral in their one-shoulder crisscross aqua dresses. Their bouquets would be plum and white, smaller versions of the dramatic rose-and-peony creation Delores had ordered for Crista. It was going to be heavy, but Delores had said with a congregation that large, people needed to see it from a distance. They could probably see it from Mars.

"The flowers are here?" asked Crista, half hoping they hadn't arrived so she wouldn't have to lug the monstrosity around.

"Yes. They're looking for you downstairs to get some pictures before you leave."

"It's time," said Crista, bracing herself.

"It's not too late," said Hadley. "We can make a break for it through the rose garden."

"You need to shut up."

He grinned. "Shutting up now."

Crista was getting married today. It might have happened fast. The ceremony might be huge. And her new family might be overwhelming. But all she had to do was put one foot in front of the other, say, "I do," and smile in all the right places.

By tonight, she'd be Mrs. Vern Gerhard. By this time tomorrow, she'd be off on a Mediterranean honeymoon.

A posh private jet would take them to a sleek private yacht for a vacation in keeping with the stature of the Gerhard family.

Hadley offered her his arm, and she took it, feeling a sudden need to hang on tight.

"I'll see you at the church," he said.

She could do this. She would do this. There was no downside. Any woman would be thrilled by such a complete and total change in her lifestyle.

Dressed in a crisp tuxedo, freshly shaved, his short hair neatly trimmed, Jackson stood outside Saint Luke's Cathedral north of Chicago in the Saturday afternoon sunshine pretending he belonged. It was a picture-perfect June wedding day. The last of the well-heeled guests had just been escorted inside, and the grooms-men now stood in a cluster on the outside stairs. Vern Gerhard was nowhere to be seen, likely locked up in an anteroom with the best man waiting for Crista Cor-day to arrive.

Jackson had learned a lot about Crista over the past three days. He'd learned she was beautiful, creative and reputedly hardworking.

As a girl, she'd grown up in a modest neighborhood, living with her single mother, her father, Trent, having visitation rights and apparently providing some small amount of financial support. She'd attended commu-nity college, taking a diploma in fine arts. It was dur-ing that time that she'd lost her mother in a car accident.

After graduation she'd found a job in women's cloth-ing in a local department store. He assumed she must have worked on her jewelry designs in her off hours.

So far, she seemed exactly as she appeared, an ordi-nary, working-class Chicago native who'd been living a perfectly ordinary life until she'd met her fiancé. The most remarkable thing about her seemed to be her father's conviction on fraud charges. Then again, maybe it wasn't so remarkable. This was Chicago, and Jackson was definitely familiar with having a convicted criminal in the family.

Vern and the Gerhards had proven harder for him to gauge. Their public and social media presence was slick and heavily controlled. Their family company, Gerhard Incorporated, was privately held, having been started as a hardware store by Vern's great-grandfather during the Depression. It now centered on commercial real estate ownership and development.

Their estimated net worth was high, but Jackson hadn't found anything illegal or shady in their business dealings. They did seem to have incredible timing, often buying up properties at fire sale prices in the months before corporate mergers, gentrification or zoning changes boosted their value. It was enough to make Jackson curious, but the individual instances weren't overly suspicious, and what he had so far didn't come close to proving they were conning Crista.

Despite Trent's suspicions, Vern Gerhard and Crista's romance seemed to be just that, a romance.

"I say more power to him." One of the groomsmen's voices carried from the cathedral staircase, catching Jackson's attention.

"I almost told her at the house," said another groomsman. This one looked younger. He had the trademark Gerhard brown eyes, but he was taller than most, younger than Vern. His flashy hairstyle made him look like he belonged in a boy band.

"Why would you do that?" asked a third. This man

was shorter, balding, and his bow tie was already askew. Jackson recognized him as a brother-in-law to Vern.

"You don't think she deserves to know?" asked the younger one.

"Who cares? She's hot," said the bald one. "That body, hoo boy."

"Such a sweet ass," said the first groomsman, grinning.

"Nice," Jackson muttered under his breath. The Gerhards might be rich, but they didn't seem to have much in the way of class.

"So, why does he need Gracie?" asked the younger groomsman, glancing around the circle for support. "He should break it off already."

"You want to stick to just one ice cream flavor?" asked the balding man.

"For the rest of your life?" asked the first groomsman.

"Some days I feel like praline pecan. Some days I feel like rocky road," said the heavyset one with a chortle.

"And *that's* why you're sleeping with Lacey Hanniberry."

"Lumpy Lacey."

The other men laughed.

"Vern hit the jackpot." The first groomsman made a rude gesture with his hips.

"On both fronts," said the bald one. "Crista's the lady, Gracie's the tramp."

"She's going to find out," said the younger man with the flashy hair.

"Not if you don't tell her she won't," said the first man, a warning in his tone.

Jackson had half a mind to tell her himself. Vern

sounded like a pig. And most of his friends didn't seem any better.

"Gracie won't last, anyway," said the heavyset man.

"Vern will trade up," said the balding one.

"Uncle Manfred's girlfriends have been twenty-five for the past thirty years."

"Wives age, girlfriends don't."

They all laughed, except for the young guy. He frowned instead. "Crista's different."

"No, she's not." The first groomsman slapped him on the back. "You're young, naive. All your girlfriends are twenty-five."

"I don't cheat on them."

"Then you're not trying hard enough."

"Get with the program."

Out of the corner of his eye, Jackson saw two white limos pull up to the curb. The groomsmen spotted them, too, and they turned to head up the wide staircase to the cathedral entrance, their voices and laughter fading with the distance.

So, Vern was cheating on Crista. It was a coldhearted and idiotic move, but it was none of Jackson's business. Maybe she knew and accepted it. Or maybe she wasn't as smart as everyone seemed to think, and she was oblivious. Or maybe—and this was a real possibility—she was only marrying the guy for his money and didn't care about his fidelity one way or the other.

The limo doors opened and a group of pretty bridesmaids spilled out of one. The driver of the other vehicle quickly hopped to the back door, helping the bride step onto the sidewalk.

Crista straightened and rose in the bright sunshine, looking absolutely stunning. Her auburn hair was swept up in braids, thick at the nape of her neck, wispy and delicate around her beautiful face. Her shoulders were bare and looked creamy smooth. The white dress was tight across her breasts and her waist, showing off an amazing figure. The lace and beading on the full skirt glittered with every little movement.

Jackson didn't normally fantasize about brides. But if he had, they'd look exactly like her. His annoyance at Vern redoubled. What was the man's problem? If Jackson had someone like Crista in his bed, he'd never so much as look at another woman.

The bridesmaids giggled and clustered around her while the drivers returned to their cars to move them from the busy street.

"This is it," said one bridesmaid, fussing with Crista's bouquet and taking a critical look at her face and hairdo.

"I'm okay?" Crista asked.

"You're perfect."

Crista drew in a deep breath.

The women started for the staircase that led to the cathedral's big front doors. Jackson's first instinct was to step forward and offer his arm, but he held back.

Crista spotted him. She looked puzzled at first, as if she was struggling to recognize him. Their gazes locked, and he felt a shot to his solar plexus.

Her eyes were green as a South Pacific sea and just as deep, flickering in the sunshine. She looked honest. She looked honorable. In that split second, he knew her father's words had been true. She wouldn't put up with a cheating husband, which meant she didn't know about Vern and Gracie.

Jackson wanted to shout at her to stop, to get out of here. She might not know it, but she was making a mistake. Deep down in his gut, he knew she was making a terrible mistake.

Maybe he should tell her the truth about Vern, just call out, right here, right now. Then at least she'd know what she was getting herself into. He told himself to do it. He owed Vern absolutely nothing. He formed the words inside his head, opened his mouth and was ready to blurt it out.

But then a bridesmaid whispered to Crista. She laughed, and her gaze broke from Jackson's, releasing him from the spell.

The women moved up the staircase, and the moment was lost.

He shook himself. It was time for him to leave. There was nothing more he could do here, nothing he could do for Trent except hope the man was wrong. The Gerhards seemed like a singularly distasteful family, and if they really were after her diamond mine, she had herself some trouble. But it wasn't Jackson's trouble to borrow. He'd done as he'd promised, and he'd found nothing concrete, nothing that said the Gerhards were nefarious criminals.

The bridesmaids filed in through the doorway, chattering among themselves. Crista hung back, touching each of her earrings, fingering her necklace then grasping her large bouquet in both hands and tipping up her chin.

Then, unexpectedly, she twisted her head to look back again. He felt that same rush of emotion tighten his chest cavity. He knew with an instant certainty that she deserved better than Vern. It might be none of his business, but surely she wouldn't tolerate a husband who'd sneak off and sleep with a string of mistresses.

The heavy door swung shut behind the bridesmaids.

Just he and Crista were left outside.

Jackson glanced around and confirmed that for these short seconds, they were alone.

Before his brain could form a thought, his feet were moving. He was striding toward her.

Her green eyes went wide, and she drew her head back in obvious surprise.

"Crista Corday?" he asked.

"Are you a friend of Vern's?" Her sexy voice seemed to strum along his nervous system.

"Not for long," he said. He scooped her into his arms and began walking.

"What?" she squeaked, one of her hands pushing on his shoulder, the other gripping the big bouquet.

"I'm not going to hurt you." He lengthened his stride to the sidewalk.

"You're not...*what* are you doing?"

"There are things you don't know about Vern."

"*Put me down!*" She started to squirm, glancing frantically around.

"I will," he promised, speeding up his pace. "In a moment."

He reached out and opened the driver's door of his SUV. He shoved her across to the passenger side. Before she had a chance to react, he jumped in behind her, cranked the engine and gunned the accelerator, peeling away from the curb, narrowly missing a taxi, which responded with a long blast from its horn.

"You can't do this," Crista cried, twisting her neck to look back at the church.

"I only want to talk."

"I'm *getting married.*"

"After you hear me out if you still want to get married, I'll take you back to him."

And, he would. Trent was a criminal. He could easily be lying about the Gerhards for reasons of his own. So, if Crista was okay with infidelity, Jackson would return her to Vern. It would go against every instinct inside him, but he'd do it.

Two

"Take me back *now*," Crista shouted at the stranger who seemed to be abducting her. Her mind raced to make some sense out of the situation.

"As soon as you hear me out." His jaw was tight, his eyes straight ahead, his hands firm on the wheel as they gathered speed.

"Who *are* you?" She struggled not to panic.

She'd always considered herself a smart, sensible, capable woman. But in this scenario she had no idea what to do.

"Jackson Rush. I'm an investigator."

"Investigating what?" She struggled to stay calm. What was he doing? Why had he taken her?

Then she saw a red light coming up. He'd have to stop for it. When he did, she'd jump from the vehicle. She quickly glanced at the passenger door to locate the handle.

She'd open the door, jump out and run to... She scanned the businesses along the section of the street. The Greek restaurant might be closed. The apartment building doors would be locked. But the drug store. That would be open, and it would be crowded. Surely one of the clerks would lend a bride a phone.

She realized she was still holding onto her bouquet, and she let it slip from her hand to the floor. She didn't need it slowing her down. Vern's mother would flip. Then again, Vern's mother, along with everyone else, was probably flipping already. Had anyone seen this man, Jackson, take her?

She surreptitiously slanted a glance his way. He was maybe thirty. He looked tough and determined, maybe a little world-weary. But there was no denying he was attractive. He was obviously fit under the tux, and very well-groomed.

The vehicle was slowing. She lifted her hand, ready to grab the handle.

But suddenly he hit the accelerator, throwing her back in her seat and sideways as he made a hard right. Another car honked as their tires squealed against the pavement.

"What are you *doing*?" she demanded.

"How well do you know Vern Gerhard?"

What a ridiculous question. "He's my fiancé."

"Would it surprise you to know he was cheating on you?"

Crista's jaw dropped. "Where did that come from?"

"Would it surprise you?" Jackson repeated.

"Vern's not cheating on me." The idea was preposterous.

Vern was sweet and kind and loyal. He made no secret of the fact that he adored Crista. They were about

to be married. And his family was extremely old-fashioned. Vern would never risk disappointing his mother
by cheating.

No, scratch that. Vern wouldn't cheat because Vern
wouldn't cheat. It had nothing to do with Delores.

"Okay," said Jackson, the skepticism clear in his
tone.

"Take me back," she said.

"I can't do that. Not yet."

"There are three hundred people in that church.
They're all waiting for me to walk down the aisle."

She could only imagine the scene as the guests grew
more restless and Vern grew more confused. She wasn't
wearing a watch, and she didn't have her cell phone.
But what time was it? Exactly how late was she to her
own wedding?

She scanned the dashboard for a clock. Traffic was
light, and Jackson seemed able to gauge the stoplights
and adjust his speed, making sure he didn't have to
come to a halt.

"Would you care if he was cheating?" asked Jackson, eyeing her quickly. "Would that be a deal breaker
for you?"

"He's not cheating." It didn't look like she'd have a
chance to bail out anytime soon. "Do you want money?
Will you call in a ransom demand? They'll probably
pay. They'll probably pay more if you take me back
there right away."

"This isn't about money."

"Then what's it about?" She struggled to keep her
tone even but panic was creeping in.

He seemed to hesitate over his answer. "You deserve
to be sure. About Vern."

"You don't even know me." She stared at him more closely. "Do you? Have we met?"

Could he be some long-lost person from her past?

"We haven't met," he said.

She racked her brain for an explanation. "Then do you know Vern? Did he do something bad to you?"

She realized she ought to be frightened. She'd been kidnapped—*kidnapped*. This stranger was holding her hostage and wouldn't let her go.

"I've never met Vern," he said.

"Then are you crazy? Though I suppose that's a stupid question. Crazy people never question their own sanity." She realized she was babbling, but she couldn't seem to help herself.

"I'm beginning to think I am," he said.

"A sure sign that you're not."

He gave a chopped laugh and seemed to drop his guard.

She tried to take advantage. "Will you let me go? Please, just pull over and drop me off. I'll find my own way back to the church."

It had to be at least fifteen minutes now. Vern would be frantic. Delores would be incensed. Unless someone saw Jackson grab her, they probably thought she ran away.

Now she wondered what Hadley was thinking. He might guess she'd taken his advice, changed her mind, that she didn't want to marry Vern after all. She scrunched her eyes shut and shook her head. How had things gotten so mixed up?

"He's cheating on you, Crista. Why would you want to marry a man who's cheating on you?"

"First of all, he's not. And…" She paused, experienced a moment of clarity. "Wait a minute. If I say I don't care if he's cheating, will you let me go?"

"If you honestly don't care and you want to marry him anyway, yeah, I'll let you go."

"Then I don't care." Why hadn't she thought of this sooner? "It's fine. No problem." She waved a dismissive hand. "He can cheat away. I still want to marry him."

"You're lying."

"I'm not." She was.

"I don't believe you."

"You've never met me. You don't know a thing about me."

He shook his head. "I can tell you have pride."

"I have no pride. Maybe I like to share. Maybe I'm into polygamy. After this wedding, Vern might find another wife. We'll all live happily ever after."

"As if."

"Let me go!"

"I'm here because somebody out there cares about you, Crista."

"I know somebody cares about me. His name is Vern Gerhard. Do you have any idea how upset he is right now?"

Jackson's tone went dry. "Maybe Gracie could console him."

The name set a shiver through Crista's chest. "*What* did you say?"

"Gracie," Jackson repeated, doing a double take at Crista's face. "You okay?"

"I'm fine. No, I'm not. I've been kidnapped!"

"Do you know someone named Gracie?"

Crista did know Gracie Stolt. Or at least she knew *of* a Gracie Stolt. Vern had once used that name during a phone call. He'd said it was business. It *had* been business, making the name irrelevant to this conversation.

"I don't know any Gracie," she said to Jackson, her tone tart.

"He's sleeping with Gracie."

"Stop saying that."

The vehicle bounced, and she grabbed the armrest to steady herself. She realized they'd turned off the main roads and onto a tree-lined lane.

A new and horrible thought crossed her mind, and her throat went dry. Was Jackson some sicko with a thing for brides?

"Are you going to hurt me?" she rasped.

"What?" He did another double take. "No. I told you. I'm not going to harm you at all."

"I bet every psychopathic murderer says that."

The corner of his mouth tipped up, but then quickly disappeared. "We have a mutual acquaintance. The person who sent me is someone who cares about you."

"Who?"

"I can't reveal my client."

"I bet every psychopathic murderer says that, too."

She was vacillating between genuine fear and disbelief that any of this could be real.

"I'm sorry you're frightened right now, but I'm not going to hurt you. You'll figure that out soon enough, I promise."

They rounded a corner, and a lake fanned out before them, the gravel beach dotted with weathered docks. He pulled to the side of a small, deserted parking lot.

"Are we there?" she asked.

"Almost." He nodded toward one of the docks.

A tall white cabin cruiser bobbed against its moor lines.

Crista shrank back against the seat, her voice going up an octave. "You're going to dump my body in the lake?"

He extracted a cell phone from his inside jacket pocket. "I'm going to call my staff."

"You have a phone?"

"Of course I have a phone."

"You should make a ransom call. My fiancé is from a rich family. They'll pay you."

At least she hoped the Gerhards would pay to get her back. She was certain Vern would be willing. His father, maybe not so much.

Jackson hated that he was frightening Crista. But he was operating on the fly here. Taking her a quarter mile offshore on Lake Michigan was the best he could come up with to keep her safe but under wraps. He wasn't about to tie her up in a basement while Mac and some of his other guys looked into Vern Gerhard's love life.

"You're going to jail, you know," she said for about the twenty-fifth time.

She stood on the deck of the boat, gazing back at the mansions along the coastline, their lights coming up as the sun sank away. Her extravagant white wedding gown rustled in the breeze. The intricate lace-and bead-covered skirt was bell shaped, billowing out from a tight waist, while the strapless top accentuated her gorgeous figure.

She was right. He was taking a very stupid risk. But the alternative had been to let the wedding go ahead. Which he could have done. In fact, he should have done. He owed nothing to her father and nothing to his own father. And Crista was all but a stranger to him. She was an intelligent adult, and she'd made her choice in Vern. He should have walked away.

"I'm hoping you won't press charges," he said, moving to stand beside her.

"In what universe would I not press charges?"

Though he knew she was frightened, her expression was defiant. He couldn't help but be impressed with her spirit.

"In the universe where I did you a favor."

"You destroyed my wedding. Do you have any idea how important this was to my mother-in-law? How much she planned and spent?"

"To your mother-in-law?"

"Yes."

"Not to you?"

Her expression faltered. "Well, me, too, of course. It was my wedding."

"It was an odd way to put it, worrying about your mother-in-law first."

"What I meant was, from my own perspective, I can get married any old time, in the courthouse, in Vegas, whatever. But she has certain expectations, a certain standing in the community. She wants to impress her friends and the rest of the family."

"She sounds charming."

"It comes with the Gerhard territory." There was a resignation to her tone.

"What about Vern? How did he feel about the opulent wedding?"

"He was all for it. He's close to his family. He wants them to be happy."

"Does he want you to be happy?"

Crista glanced sharply up at Jackson. "Yes, he wants

me to be happy. But he knows I don't sweat the small stuff."

Jackson lifted a brow. "The small stuff being your own wedding?"

She shrugged her bare shoulders, and he was suddenly seized by an urge to run his palms over them, to test the smoothness of her skin. Was she cold out here on the lake?

"It'll work just as well with three hundred people in the room as it would with two witnesses and a judge."

Jackson stifled a chuckle. "You sure don't sound like the average bride."

Her tone turned dry. "The average bride doesn't have a five-hundred-dollar wedding bouquet."

"Seriously?"

"I don't know for sure, but I think that's in the ballpark."

Jackson drew back to take in the length of her. "And the dress?"

She spread her arms. "Custom-made in Paris."

"You flew to Paris for a wedding dress."

"Don't be ridiculous. The designer flew to Chicago."

This time Jackson did laugh. "You have got to be kidding."

"And that was only the start. I'm wearing antique diamonds." She tilted her head to show him her ears.

He wanted to kiss her neck. It was ridiculous, given the circumstances, but there was something incredibly sensual about the curve of her neck, the line of her jaw, the lush red of her lips.

"And you should see my underwear," she said.

Their gazes met. She took in his stare and obviously saw a flare of desire. Those gorgeous green eyes widened in surprise, and she took a step back.

He wanted to tell her he'd give pretty much anything to see her underwear. But he kept his mouth firmly shut.

"You wouldn't," she said, worry in her tone.

"I wouldn't," he affirmed. "I won't. I'm not going to try anything out of line." He turned his attention to the shoreline.

"Will you take me back?" she asked.

"I doubt there's anybody left at the church."

"They'll be crazy with worry," she said. "They'll have called the police by now."

"The police won't take a missing-person report for twenty-four hours."

"You don't know my future in-laws."

"I know the Chicago Police Department."

"Why are you doing this?"

"I was hired to look into Vern Gerhard's integrity."

"By who?"

Jackson shook his head. "I have a strict policy of client confidentiality."

Given their understandably fractured relationship, bringing Trent's name into it would be the fastest way to completely lose her trust. Not that he'd blame her. He felt the same about anything his own father touched.

"But you don't have a strict policy against kidnapping innocent people?" she asked.

"To be honest, this is the first time it's come up."

"I *am* going to press charges." It was clear she was serious.

There was no denying that the situation had spiraled out of control. But there was also nothing to do but keep moving forward. If he took her back now, the Gerhards would definitely have him arrested. His only hope was to find proof of Vern's infidelity and turn Crista against her fiancé.

His phone rang. He kept eye contact with her as he reached for it.

It was Mac, his right-hand man.

"Hey," Jackson answered.

"Everything okay so far?" asked Mac.

"Yeah." Jackson turned away from Crista and moved along the deck toward the bridge. "You come up with anything?"

"Rumors, yes. But nothing that gives us proof. Norway's looking into Gracie."

"Pictures would be good."

"Videotape better."

"I'd take videotape," said Jackson. "Is somebody on the family?"

"I am."

"And?"

"They've contacted the police, but they're being waved off until morning. I guess runaway brides aren't that unusual."

"If Vern Gerhard is a typical example of our gender, I don't blame them."

Mac coughed out a laugh.

"I guess we've got till morning," said Jackson.

It was less time than he would have liked. But that's what happened when you threw a plan together at the last minute.

"And then?" asked Mac. "Have you thought through what happens in the morning?"

He had, and most of the options were not good. "We better have something concrete by then."

"Otherwise she's a liability," said Mac.

Jackson had to agree. "At that point, she's going to be a huge liability."

Crista was predictably angry at having her posh wedding ruined. If they didn't find something to incriminate Vern, Jackson's career if not his freedom would be at stake.

He heard a sudden splash behind him.

He spun to find the deck empty, Crista gone. His gaze moved frantically from corner to corner as he rushed to the stern and spotted her in the water. "You gotta be kidding me!"

"What?" asked Mac.

"Call you back." Jackson dropped his phone.

She was flailing in the choppy waves, obviously hampered by the voluminous white dress. She gasped and went under.

He immediately tossed two life jackets overboard, as close to her as he could.

"Grab one!" he shouted. Then he stripped off his jacket, kicked off his shoes and dived in.

The water closed icy cold around him. He surfaced and gasped in a big breath. She was twenty feet away, and he kicked hard. He dug in with his arms, propelling himself toward her.

When he looked up again, she was gone. He twisted his head, peering in all directions, spotting a wisp of white below the surface. He dived under, groping in the dark until he caught hold of her arm. He clamped his hand tight and hauled her upward, breaking the surface and wrapping his arm firmly around her chest.

She coughed and sputtered.

"Relax," he told her. "Just relax and let me do the work."

She coughed again.

He grabbed one of the life jackets and tucked it beneath her. The boat was close, but the water was frigid.

He wasn't going to be able to swim for long. Her teeth were already chattering.

He found another life jacket and looped it around the arm that supported her. He used his legs and free arm to move them through the water.

"You okay?" he asked her. "You breathing?"

She nodded against his chest.

"Don't fight me," he cautioned.

"I won't," she rasped.

The side of the boat loomed closer. He aimed for the stern where there was a small swimming platform. It was a relief to grasp on to something solid. His muscles throbbed from the effects of the cold water, and his limbs were starting to shake.

He unceremoniously cupped her rear end and shoved her onto the platform. She scrambled up, her dress catching and tearing. He kept her braced until she was stable. Then he looped both forearms over the platform and hoisted himself up, sitting on the edge, dragging in deep breaths.

"What the heck?" he demanded.

She was breathing hard. "I thought I could make it."

"To the beach?"

"It's not that far."

"It's a quarter mile. And you're dressed in an anchor."

"The fabric is light."

"Maybe when it's bone-dry." He reached up and pulled himself to his feet. His legs trembled, and his knees felt weak, but he put an arm around her waist and lifted her up beside him.

With near-numb fingers, he released the catch on the deck gate and swung it open.

"Careful," he cautioned as he propelled her back onto the deck.

She held on and stepped shakily forward. "It tangled around my legs."

"You could have killed us both." He followed her.

"It'd serve you right."

"To be *dead*? You'd be dead, too."

"I'm going to be dead anyway."

"What?" He was baffled now.

She was shivering. "I heard you on the phone. You said tomorrow morning I'd be a liability. We both know what that means."

"One of us obviously doesn't."

"Don't bother to deny it."

"Nobody's killing anyone." He gazed out at the dark water. "Despite your best attempt."

"You can't let me live. I'll turn you in. You'll go to jail."

"You might not turn me in."

"Would you actually believe me if I said I wouldn't?"

"At the moment, no."

Right now, she was having a perfectly normal reaction to the circumstances. Proof of the truth might mitigate her anger eventually, but they didn't have that yet.

"Then that was a really stupid statement," she said.

"What I am going to prove is that I mean you no harm."

It was the best he could come up with for the moment. The breeze was chilling, and he ushered her past the bridge, opening the door to the cabin.

"How are you going to do that?"

"For starters by not harming you. Let's find you something dry."

She glared at him. "I'm not taking off my dress."

He pointed inside. "You can change in the head—the bathroom. I've got some T-shirts on board and maybe some sweatpants, though they'd probably drop right off you."

"This is your boat?"

"Of course it's my boat. Whose boat did you think it was?"

She passed through the door and stopped between the sofa and the kitchenette. "I thought maybe you stole it."

"I'm not a thief."

"You're a kidnapper."

He realized she'd made a fair point. "Yeah, well, that's the sum total of my criminal activity to date." He started working on his soggy tie. "If you let me get past you, I'll see what I can find."

She shrank out of his way against the counter.

He turned sideways to pass her, and their thighs brushed together. She arched her back to keep her breasts from touching his chest. It made things worse, because her wet cleavage swelled above the snug, stiff fabric.

Reaction slammed through his body, and he faltered, unable to stop himself from staring. She was soaked to the skin, her auburn hair plastered to her head, her makeup smeared. And yet she was still the most beautiful woman he'd ever seen.

"Jackson," she said, her voice coming out a whisper.

He lifted his gaze to meet hers. It was all he could do to keep his hands by his sides. He wanted to smooth her hair, brush the droplets from her cheeks and run his thumb across her lips.

"Thank you," she said.

The words took him by surprise. "You're welcome," he automatically answered.

For a minute, it seemed that neither of them could break eye contact. Longing roiled inside him. He wanted to kiss her. He wanted to do so much more. And he wanted it very, very badly.

Finally, she looked away. "You better, uh…"

"Yeah," he said. "I'd better." He moved, but the touch of her thighs made him feel like he'd been branded.

Crista reached and twisted. She stretched her arms in every direction, but no matter how she contorted, she couldn't push the tiny buttons through the loops on the back of her dress.

"Come on," she muttered. Then she whacked her elbow against a small cabinet. "Ouch!"

"You okay?" came Jackson's deep voice.

He was obviously only inches from the other side of the small door, and the sound made her jerk back. Her hip caught the corner of the vanity, and she sucked in a sharp breath.

"Fine," she called back.

"I'm getting changed out here."

"Thanks for the warning." An unwelcome picture bloomed in her mind of Jackson peeling off his dress shirt, revealing what had to be washboard abs and muscular shoulders. She'd clung to him in the ocean and again climbing onto the boat. She'd felt what was under his dress shirt, and her brain easily filled in the picture.

She shook away the vision and redoubled her efforts with the buttons. But it wasn't going to happen. She couldn't get out of the dress alone. She had two choices—stay in the soaking-wet garment or ask him for help. Both were equally disagreeable.

She caught a glimpse of herself in the small mirror. The wedding gown was stained and torn. She crouched a little, cringing at the mess of her hair. It was stringy and lopsided. If she didn't undo the braids and rinse out the mess from the lake water she'd probably have to shave it off in the morning.

"Are you decent?" she called through the door.

"Sure," he answered.

She opened the small door, stepped over the sill, and Jackson filled her vision. The cabin was softly lit around him. His hair was damp, and his chest was bare. A pair of worn gray sweatpants hung on his hips. As she'd expected, his abs were washboard hard.

"What happened?" he asked, taking in her dress.

"I can't reach the buttons."

He gave an eye roll and pulled a faded green T-shirt over his head. "I'll give you a hand."

She turned her back and steeled herself for his touch. The only reason she was letting him near her was that it was foolish to stay cold and uncomfortable in a ruined dress. She told herself that if he was going to kill her, he would have just let her go under. Instead, he'd saved her life.

His footfalls were muffled against the teak floor as he came up behind her. The sound stopped, and he drew in an audible breath. Then his fingertips grazed her skin above the top button, sending streaks of sensation up her spine. Her muscles contracted in reaction.

What was the matter with her? She wasn't attracted to him. She was appalled by him. She wanted to get away from him, to never see him again.

But as his deft fingers released each button, there was no denying her growing arousal. It had to be some pathetic version of Stockholm syndrome. If she'd paid more attention in her psychology elective, she might know how to combat it.

The dress came loose, and she clasped her forearms against her chest to keep it in place.

"That should do it," he said.

There was a husky timbre to his voice—a sexy rasp that played havoc with her emotions.

"Thanks," she said before she could stop herself. "I mean…" She turned to take the sentiment back, and her gaze caught with his. "That is…"

They stared at each other.

"I don't usually do this," he said.

She didn't know what he meant. He didn't usually kidnap women, or he didn't unbutton their wedding gowns?

She knew she should ask. No, she shouldn't ask. She should move now, lock herself in the bathroom until her emotions came under control.

But he slowly lifted his hand. His fingertips grazed her shoulder. Then his palm cradled her neck, slipping up to her hairline. The touch was smooth and warm, his obvious strength couched by tenderness.

She couldn't bring herself to pull away. In fact, it was a fight to keep from leaning into his caress.

He dipped his head.

She knew what came next. Anybody would know what came next.

His lips touched hers, kissing her gently, testing her texture and then her taste. Arousal instantly flooded her body. He stepped forward, his free arm going around her waist, settling at the small of her back, strong and hot against her exposed skin.

He pressed harder, kissed her deeper. She met his tongue, opening, drowning in the sweet sensations that enveloped her.

Good thing she didn't marry Vern today.

The thought brought her up short.

She let out a small cry and jerked away.

What was the matter with her?

"What are you doing?" she demanded, tearing from his hold.

Her dress slipped, and she struggled to catch the bodice. She was a second too late, and she flashed him her bare breasts.

His eyes glowed, and his nostrils flared.

"Back off," she ordered, quickly covering up.

"You kissed me too," he pointed out.

"You took me by surprise."

"We both know that's a lie."

"We do not," she snapped, taking a step away.

"Whatever you say."

"I'm *engaged.*"

"So I've heard," he drawled. "Are you sure that's what you want?"

She couldn't seem to frame an answer.

If not for Jackson, she'd already be married to Vern. They'd be at the reception, cutting the enormous cake and dancing to Strauss's *Snowdrops*, Delores's favorite waltz. Crista's knees suddenly felt weak, and she sat down on the padded bench beside her.

"The thought of being married makes you feel faint?" Jackson asked.

"I'm worried about my mother-in-law. I can't even imagine how she reacted. All those guests. All that planning. What did they do when I didn't show up? Did they all just go home?"

"You're not worried about Vern?"

"Yes, I'm worried about Vern. Quit putting words in my mouth."

"You never said his name."

"Vern, Vern, Vern. I'm worried sick about Vern. He's going through hell." Then a thought struck her. "You should call him. *I* should call him. I can at least let him know I'm all right."

"I can't let you use my phone."

"Because then they'd discover it was you. And they'd arrest you. And you'd go to jail. You know, sooner than you're already going to jail after I tell the police everything you did." Crista paused. Maybe she wouldn't tell them *everything*. Better to keep certain missteps off the public record.

"I've got five guys working on this." Jackson lowered himself to the bench opposite, the compact table between them.

"Five guys working on what?" Her curiosity was piqued.

"Vern's infidelity."

"Vern wasn't unfaithful."

Jackson smirked. "Right. And you never kissed me too."

Crista wasn't about to lie again. "Just tell me what you want. Whatever is going on here, let's please get this over with so I can go home."

"I want you to wait here with me while I find out exactly what your husband-to-be has been up to with Gracie."

"Gracie's a business acquaintance." Crista immediately realized her slipup.

Jackson caught it, too. "So, you do know her."

Crista wasn't about to renew the debate. She knew what she knew, and she trusted Vern.

"Why are you doing this?" she asked Jackson again.

"So you can decide whether or not you want to marry him."

"I *do* want to marry him."

His gaze slipped downward, and she realized her grip on her dress had relaxed. She was showing cleavage—a lot of cleavage. She quickly adjusted.

"Maybe," he said softly.

"There's no maybe about it."

"What's the harm in waiting?" he asked, sounding sincere. "The wedding's already ruined."

"Thanks to you."

"My point is there's no harm in waiting a few more hours."

"Except for my frantic fiancé."

Jackson seemed to think for a moment. "I can have someone call him, tell him you're okay."

"From a pay phone?" she mocked.

"Who uses pay phones? We've got plenty of burner phones."

"Of course you do."

"You want me to call?"

"Yes!" But then she thought about it. "No. Hang on. What are you going to tell him?"

"What do you want me to tell him?"

"The truth."

"Yeah, that's not going to happen."

"Then tell him I'm okay. Tell him something unexpected came up. I'm…uh…" She bit down on her lower lip. "I don't know. Other than the truth, what can I possibly say that doesn't sound terrible?"

"You got me."

"He'll think I got cold feet."

"He might."

"No, he won't." She shook her head firmly. Vern knew her better than that. He knew she was committed to their marriage.

But Jackson would never send a message that incriminated himself. And anything else could make it sound like it had been her decision to run off. Maybe it was better to keep silent.

"How long do you think this will take?" she asked. "To clear Vern's name?"

Jackson gave a shrug. "It could go pretty fast. My guys are good."

Crista rose to her feet. "Then don't call him. I'm going to change."

"Good idea."

"It doesn't mean I've capitulated."

"I took it to mean you wanted to be dry."

"That's exactly what it means."

"Okay," he agreed easily.

She turned away from his smug expression, gripping the front of her ruined wedding dress, struggling to hold on to some dignity as she made her way into the bathroom. She could feel his gaze on her back, taking in the expanse of bare skin. He knew she wasn't wearing a bra, and he could probably see the white lace at the top of her panties.

A rush of heat coursed through her. She told herself it was anger. She didn't care where he looked, or what he thought. It was the last he'd see of her that was remotely intimate.

Three

Jackson recognized Mac's number and put his phone to his ear. "Find something?"

"Norway talked to the girl," said Mac.

"Did she admit to the affair?"

"She says there's nothing between them. But she's lying. And she's doing it badly. Norway got thirty seconds alone with her phone and grabbed some photos."

That was encouraging. "Anything incriminating?"

"No nudity, but they do look intimate. Gerhard's got an arm around her shoulders, and his expression says he slept with her. We're combing through social media now."

"Good. Keep me posted."

"How are things at your end?"

Crista emerged from the bathroom. Her hair was still wet but combed straight. She'd washed her face, and she was dressed in Jackson's white and maroon U of Chicago soccer jersey. It hung nearly to her knees, which were bare, as were her calves.

"Pants didn't fit?" he asked.

"Huh?" asked Mac.

"Fell off," she said.

"Stay safe," Jackson said to Mac, setting down his phone.

"Who's that?" asked Crista, moving to the sofa. She took the end opposite to Jackson and tucked the hem of the jersey over her knees.

"Mac."

"He works for your agency?"

"He does."

She nodded. She looked curious but stayed silent.

"Are you afraid to ask?" he guessed.

She flicked back her damp hair. "I'm not afraid to ask anything."

"They found some pictures of Vern and Gracie."

"You're bluffing."

"They're not specifically incriminating—"

"I know they're not."

"But they are suggestive of more than a business relationship."

"If suggestive is all you've got, then let me go."

"It's all we've got *so far.*" He glanced at his watch. "We've only been chasing this lead for five hours."

She heaved an exaggerated sigh.

"You hungry?" he asked.

He was, and he doubted brides were inclined to eat heartily before their weddings.

"No," she said.

"You really need to stop lying."

"*You're* criticizing *my* behavior?"

"You're not going to help anything by starving."

He rose, taking the few steps to the small kitchen and popping open a high cupboard.

"You're not going to make me like you," she said from behind him.

"Why would I want to make you like me?"

He wanted to convince her not to marry Vern. No, scratch that. He couldn't care less if she married Vern. No, scratch that, too. Vern didn't deserve her. If Jackson was sure of one thing in all this, it was that Vern didn't deserve a woman like Crista.

"To make me more docile and easy to manipulate."

Jackson located a stray bag of tortilla chips. "Docile? You? Are you kidding me?"

Her tone turned defensive. "I'm really quite easy to get along with. I mean, under normal circumstances."

He also found a jar of salsa. It wasn't much, but it would keep them from starving. If they were lucky, they'd find a few cans of beer in the mini fridge.

He turned back.

She froze, her expression a study in guilt, his phone pressed to her ear.

He swore, dropping the food, taking two swift steps to grab it from her. How could he have made such an idiotic mistake?

"Nine-one-one operator," came a female voice through the phone. "What is your emergency?"

He hit the end button. "What did you do?"

"Tried to get help." Her words were bold, but she shrank back against the sofa.

Jackson hit the speed dial for Mac.

"Yeah?" Mac answered immediately.

"I have to move. This phone is compromised. Tuck's dock, zero eight hundred."

"Roger that," said Mac.

Jackson pushed open a window and tossed the phone overboard.

"That was stupid," he said to Crista.

"I was trying to escape. How was that stupid?"

"*You* were reckless. *I* was stupid."

He grasped her arm and pulled her to her feet.

"Hey," she cried.

"Listen, I'm still not going to hurt you, but you had no way of knowing that for sure. I could have been a vengeful jerk." He tugged her to the bridge, holding fast to her upper arm while he started the engine and engaged the anchor winch.

Her tone turned mulish. "I had to try."

"I shouldn't have given you the chance."

"You let your guard down."

"I did. And that was stupid."

Not to mention completely unprofessional. He wasn't sure what had distracted him. Their kiss? Her legs? The sight of her in his jersey?

He'd have to worry about it later. Right now, he couldn't take a chance on an overzealous 911 operator tracing their location. Anchor up, he opened the throttle, and they surged forward.

She swayed, but he held her steady.

"You were trying to be nice," she said.

He struggled not to laugh at that. "You're trying to make me feel better about being stupid?"

"I'm saying… I'm not unappreciative of you offering me something to eat."

"Well, I'm definitely unappreciative of you compromising our location."

He set a course north along the coastline. His friend

Tuck Tucker owned a beach house north of the city. Tuck wouldn't mind Jackson using his dock. He might mind the kidnapping part, but Jackson didn't plan to mention that. And if Mac and the others didn't come through with proof positive by morning, Tuck's reaction would be the least of Jackson's worries.

"Where are we going?" Crista asked.

Jackson did chuckle at that. "Yeah, sure. I'm going to tell you."

"It's not like we still have a phone." As she spoke, her gaze flicked to the radio.

"I'll be disconnecting the battery to that long before I take my eyes off you," he told her.

"What are you talking about?"

"You just looked at the radio. You might as well be wearing a neon sign that says it's your next move."

She drew an exasperated sigh and shifted her feet.

"You probably don't want to consider a life of crime," he said.

She lifted her chin and gave her damp hair a little toss. "I'm surprised you did."

"It's been a surprising day."

"Not exactly what I expected, either."

He'd have to hand her the win on that one.

He switched screens on the GPS, orienting himself to the shoreline.

"I'm hoping you'll thank me later," he said.

"Hoping? You don't seem as confident as before."

"The stakes just keep getting higher and higher. Now we're headed for the state line."

Her attention swung from the windshield to him. "You're taking me to *Wisconsin*?"

"What's wrong with Wisconsin?"

"It's a long way from Chicago. Why are you taking

me there? What's happening?" She struggled to get away from him.

He regretted frightening her again. They weren't really going all the way to Wisconsin.

"I didn't plan to grab you today," he told her. "I was only there to get a look at Gerhard."

"Why?"

"To take his measure."

"I mean why do you care about us at all?"

"It's a job."

"Who hired you?"

"It doesn't matter. What matters to you is that your fiancé is already having an affair. You can't marry a man like that." Jackson wasn't ready to tell her more. Mention of her father would likely alienate her further. He didn't yet have proof of Trent's accusations. And if she was having trouble accepting that Vern would cheat, she'd never believe he was conning her.

"He's not like that. I don't know where you even came up with that idea."

She'd stopped struggling against his grip, and that was good. Her fear seemed to have been replaced by anger. Jackson's guilt eased off.

"Wedding guests," he said, opening the throttle to increase their speed. It was a clear, relatively calm night, thank goodness. They needed to put distance between them and the position where Crista had made the call.

"*My* wedding guests?"

"Technically, I would say they were Vern's wedding guests. They seemed to know him, and they were joking about his relationship with Gracie. I realized I couldn't in good conscience let you marry him, so I took the opportunity and grabbed you."

She was silent for a moment. "So this isn't so much crime as altruism."

"Yes. The easiest thing for me would have been to walk away."

"You can still walk away."

"We're on a boat."

"Swim away, then. Or drop me off onshore and drive away—motor away? Float away? What do you call it?"

"Navigate away. And no, I'm not dropping you off onshore." He made a show of looking her up and down, enjoying the view far too much. "You're not dressed, for one thing."

"I'll put my wedding dress back on. It might be uncomfortable, but it's better than staying here."

"I'd get thrown in jail," he said.

"Darn right. But that's going to happen anyway."

"Not for a few hours." And hopefully not ever, although Jackson's worry factor was steadily rising.

"How long until we get there?" she asked.

"Get where?"

"To the secret location, wherever it is you're taking me. How long until we stop navigating?"

"Why?"

"Because I'm hungry."

"Oh, now you're hungry. Well, you're going to have to wait."

"I can eat while you navigate."

"I'm not letting go of you."

"I'm not going to jump."

"That's what I thought last time."

"We're way too far from shore."

"Yeah, but I'm sure you've got another brilliant plan in mind already. Sabotage the engine, harpoon me from behind."

"You have harpoons on board?"

"Give me strength," he muttered.

She leaned close to him. "Am I annoying you? Frustrating you?"

"Yes on both counts."

Her argumentative nature was annoying, but his frustration came from a whole other place. She was stimulating and exciting. She was a beautiful, feisty, apparently complex and intelligent woman, and he was battling hard against his sexual attraction to her. He didn't want to be rushing from a crime scene with her as his captive, contemplating the best way to stay out of jail. He wanted to be on a date with her, somewhere great in the city, contemplating how best to get her into his bed.

"There's a simple solution," she told him.

It took a second for him to get his brain back on track. "Let you go?" he guessed.

"Bingo."

"Not until we meet up with Mac tomorrow."

"You'll let me go then?"

He knew he was being cornered, but there really was no choice. He could only hope Mac could come up with definitive proof by morning.

"Yes," said Jackson.

Crista's mouth curved into a dazzling smile. They hit a swell, and she pressed against him. Her curves were soft, and her scent was fresh. For a moment the risk of jail seemed almost worth it.

When Crista awoke, she was disoriented. It took a few seconds to realize the warm body beside her wasn't Vern. She was in bed with someone bigger, harder, with a deeper breathing pattern and an earthier scent. And the bed was moving beneath them.

Then reality came back in a rush. Long after midnight, she'd given in and laid down on the bed in the bow of Jackson's boat. He was still up, and she'd hugged one edge of the massive, triangular shape in case he decided to join her. At some point he obviously had, and in her sleep she must have moved to the middle.

Now she was cradled by his strong arm, hers thrown across his chest. And her leg…uh-oh. Her leg was draped across his thighs. The jersey had ridden up to her waist. Luckily, he was wearing sweatpants. Otherwise, there'd be nothing between them but the lacy silk of her white panties.

She knew she should move. She had to move. And she needed to do it before he woke up and caught her in such a revealing position. Now that she thought about it, she should have recoiled from him the second she was conscious.

Staying put like this was bad. The fact that she liked it was even worse. She was an engaged woman. She was all but married. She had absolutely no business enjoying the intimate embrace of another man, no matter how fit his body, no matter how handsome his face and no matter how sexy his warm palm felt against her hip.

It was all she could do not to groan out loud.

Jackson moved and she drew a sharp breath.

"Hey, there," he whispered lazily in her ear, obviously only half-awake himself, obviously believing she was someone else.

Then he kissed her hairline.

"I—" she began. But he kissed her mouth. And his arms closed around her.

Before she could gather her wits enough to struggle,

the kiss deepened. A fog of desire invaded her brain, blocking out the real world.

He was one fantastic kisser.

His hand slipped down to cradle her rear. Pulling her to him, his thigh wedged between her legs. Arousal fanned through her, hot, heavy and demanding.

She had to make this stop. She so had to shut this down.

"Jackson," she gasped. "I'm not your date. Wake up. It's me. It's Crista."

"I know." He drew back, gazing at her with dark eyes. "I know who you are."

"But—"

"And you know I'm not Gerhard."

She wanted to deny it. She desperately wanted to lie and say that, of course, she'd thought he was her fiancé. What kind of a woman would behave like this with another man? But she couldn't bring herself to lie, not with his sharp stare only inches away, and their hearts beating together.

"I was confused," she replied instead.

He answered with a knowing smile. "Confused about what?"

"Who you were."

He shook his head. "Crista, Crista. There's no real harm in not being truthful with me. But I hope you're being honest with yourself."

"I am being honest with myself."

"You claim you love Gerhard, yet you're in bed with a stranger."

"I'm not in bed with you." She immediately realized how ridiculous the protest sounded. "I mean, not like that. We didn't... We aren't..."

He glanced down between them, noting without words that they were in each other's arms.

She quickly pulled back, wriggling to get away from him.

A pained expression came over his face. "Uh, Crista, don't—"

"What?" Had she hurt him?

"The way you're moving."

And then she realized what he meant. They might be mostly dressed, but she could feel every nuance of his body. Raw arousal coursed through her all over again. She felt her face heat in embarrassment.

"However you have to move. Whatever you have to do. Just do it," she demanded hoarsely.

He cupped a palm under her knee, lifting her leg from his body and lowering it to the mattress. But his hand lingered on her thigh.

She closed her eyes, steeling herself. What was the matter with her? "Please," she whispered.

"You're going to have to be more specific." His husky voice amped up her arousal.

"We can't." But she wanted to. She couldn't remember ever wanting a man so intensely.

"We won't," he said and gathered her into his arms all over again.

She didn't protest. Instead, she reveled in the security of his strength. Yesterday had been a nightmare of fear, disappointment and confusion. It had all been Jackson's fault. But for some reason that didn't seem to matter. He was still a comfort.

"Mac will be here in a few minutes," said Jackson.

"Is he going to swim?" she asked.

"I docked the boat last night after you fell asleep."

"You mean I could have escaped?"

"You'd have had to get out of my bed without waking me. But, yeah, you could have escaped."

Crista heaved a sigh. "This isn't normal. My reaction to these circumstances," she said.

"It doesn't feel normal to me, either." He scooted to the end of the bed and stood.

"Jackson?" A man's voice came from beyond the small hatch door.

She jerked back, quickly adjusting her jersey over her thighs.

"We'll be right out," Jackson called. To Crista he said, "You didn't do anything wrong."

"Yes, I did."

He was right about one thing—she should stop lying to herself. She might love Vern, but she'd just kissed the heck out of another man. Maybe fear and stress had combined to mess with her hormones, but what she'd done was absolutely, fundamentally wrong.

Jackson slipped a T-shirt over his head. "Forget about it."

"Are you really going to let me go?" She forced herself to think ahead.

If she could make a phone call, Vern would pick her up. She didn't have her purse, no cash or credit cards or her phone. She'd have to change back into her ruined wedding dress before he got here. Man, was he going to be ticked off about that.

"After you look at what Mac found, yes, I'll let you go."

"Good." She struggled to summon her pride as she rose from the bed.

She followed Jackson up a couple of steps and ducked through the hatch to the main cabin. There she found Mac, a tall, bulky man with broad shoulders, who had a heavy brow and a military hairstyle. Jackson looked almost urbane by comparison. The contrast to Vern would be startling.

"Mac," said Jackson with a nod. "This is Crista Corday."

"Miss Corday," said Mac. His voice was as rugged as his appearance.

"I think we can skip the formality of *Miss* Corday, since you participated in my kidnapping."

"Mac had nothing to do with it," said Jackson.

"He does now," said Crista. She was telling Vern and the police everything. Jackson and his gang of men should not be allowed to roam free.

"I've got the photos," said Mac, stepping forward.

He held out his phone so she could see the screen. The first one was taken on a busy street. It was Vern, all right. Despite herself, she leaned in for a closer look.

He walking side by side with a woman, presumably Gracie. They seemed to be exiting a restaurant. The woman was tall, with a bouncy mane of wavy blond hair. Her makeup was dark—thick, sparkly liner and a coating of mascara emphasizing her bright blue eyes. Her lips were full, her bust fuller, and her waist was tiny beneath a white tank top. The next photo showed that she wore blue leather pants and black, spike–heeled ankle boots.

"They're just walking," said Crista.

She'd allow that Gracie didn't look like your average commercial real estate client, but looks could be deceiving. One thing was for certain, she was a polar opposite of Crista.

"Wait for it," said Mac. He scrolled to another picture.

Here they were holding hands, then cuddling, then

Vern was kissing her on the cheek. It was persuasive, but Crista had played with Photoshop software. She knew that pictures could be manipulated. There were also other logical problems.

"Why would he marry me?" she asked.

Gracie was drop-dead, glamour-magazine, movie star–material stunning.

"What do you mean?" asked Jackson, looking genuinely puzzled.

Crista gestured to the photo. "If there's really something romantic between them, why not marry her? She's a knockout. And he seems to like her well enough." The two were smiling and laughing in most of the pictures.

Both Mac and Jackson were frowning at her.

"What?" she asked, looking from one to the other.

"He wants you," said Jackson.

"Which means he isn't involved with her," Crista said slowly, making sure he could understand each of her words.

"Look at this," said Mac.

He produced a picture where the two were embracing. It was nighttime, and they were dressed differently. It had been taken in front of a hotel.

"April of this year," said Mac. "It's date stamped."

Crista would admit it looked damning. *If* she believed it hadn't been altered, and *if* she believed the date stamp was valid. She was about to mount another argument in Vern's defense when she realized this was her ticket home. If Jackson thought he'd won, he'd let her go.

She gave herself a moment. She had to deliver this just right.

She took the phone from Mac's hand. She stared at the photo for a long time, pretending she was having an emotional reaction. Then she gripped the back of the bench seat that curved around the table. She lowered herself down.

"It looks bad," she said in a hushed voice.

"It is what it seems," said Mac. "I also have some emails."

Crista gave what she hoped was a shaky nod, still playacting. As if emails weren't even easier to fake than photos.

She made a show of swallowing, then she set the phone down on the table. She tried to put a catch into her voice. "I guess you were right."

"I wish I could say I was sorry."

"Don't you start lying."

To her surprise, Jackson put a comforting hand on her shoulder. "He doesn't deserve you, Crista."

"I never would have believed it," she said. "He cheated on me. He's been cheating on me the entire time. I'm such an idiot." For good measure, she pulled off her engagement ring and squeezed it in her palm.

"It's not your fault," said Jackson.

She didn't answer. If she had Jackson convinced that she'd bought his story, it was time to shut up and let it lay. It was also time to get herself out of here and back to Vern. He had to be frantic. She'd reassure him she was safe, and then she'd tell him everything. Jackson and Mac deserved whatever they got.

"Will you let me go now?" she asked.

She could feel their hesitation, but she was afraid to look up and gauge their expressions. Had she seemed too easy to convince? She hoped she hadn't overplayed her hand.

It was Jackson who spoke. "I'll drive you home."

Four

Crista had asked to be taken directly to the Gerhard mansion. Fine by Jackson. He looked forward to seeing the expression on Gerhard's face when she dumped him.

Once she'd broken it off, he'd report the success to Colin and Trent and go back to his regular life. At least, he ought to go directly back to his regular life. But he wasn't sure how quickly he wanted to walk away from her.

He found himself strongly attracted to her. But more than that, he was intrigued by her. She couldn't have had an easy life. Her father was a criminal like Jackson's. Yet, here she was, running a business, hobnobbing with Chicago's elite, almost marrying into one of the city's wealthy families.

She was obviously a survivor, and from what he'd seen of her, she was tough. She'd jumped into the bay, for goodness' sake, planning to swim for it to save herself. Okay, so maybe she was more reckless than clever. But the same could be said of him.

"Their driveway is the next right," she said.

She'd redressed in her damp wedding gown, which was now stark against the black leather seat of the Rush Investigations SUV. Jackson appreciated the drama of the visual—breaking your engagement in a ruined wedding gown—but he doubted she was thinking about that. She likely just wanted to get it over with. He couldn't say he blamed her.

He swung the vehicle into the driveway, passing a pair of brick pillars. They had lions on them. Who did that? Then he steered around the curves of a smooth, oak-lined driveway.

A quarter mile in, the mansion came into view. It was a rambling stone building, three stories high, sprawling in the center of manicured lawns and colorful flower beds. The driveway circled around a cherub fountain. Water spurted from three statues, foaming into a concrete pond.

"I should tell you," said Crista, her tone flat as he pulled to the curb and stopped in front of the grand staircase. "Just so you understand what's coming next." She angled her body to look at him. "I didn't buy it, not for a second."

He shifted to Park, his brain sorting through her words for some kind of logic. "Buy what?"

"The fake pictures of Vern. I'm sure the fake emails were just as creative."

Jackson saw where she was going, and it was nowhere good.

"I'm turning you in," she continued. Then she made a show of shoving her engagement ring back on her fin-

ger. "I'm telling them everything, and I'm not sorry."
She swung open the door.

He lunged for her, but the shoulder belt brought him
up short.

"Don't do that." He tore off his seat belt and leaped
out of the car.

She moved fast considering her spiky shoes and the
awkward dress. He rushed to catch up with her.

"They weren't fake," he said, kicking himself for
having been taken in like a chump. He'd let his mind
get ahead of events instead of properly focusing on
the moment. He'd let himself project forward, debating whether to offer her comfort right away or wait a
decent period of time before asking her out on a date.
Distracted by his attraction to her, he'd missed the signs
that she was lying.

At the top of the stairs, she rounded on him. "You
think I don't know my own fiancé."

"Crista—"

"No."

"Crista?" A man spoke from the doorway behind her.

"Vern," she gasped in obvious relief, a smile coming over her face.

Her steps quickened, and her arms went out, obviously expecting to rush into his embrace.

But Gerhard was frowning.

"Wait until I tell—" she began.

"What were you *thinking*?" he demanded on a roar.
"And who is this guy?"

She stopped short. Jackson's instincts told him to
leave. His duty was done. He was risking arrest and
imprisonment by staying.

"Your dress is absolutely ruined." Gerhard gestured
to the soiled and torn gown.

And your fiancée is safe, Jackson wanted to shout out.

Crista drew back, obviously shocked by the reaction. "I—"

"Do you have any idea what Mother has been through?" asked Gerhard.

Jackson waited for Crista to say that she'd been through something, too. He took a reflexive step away, telling himself to make good his escape before she could tell the story of how she'd been kidnapped and held against her will.

"Mother was *mortified*," said Vern. "She nearly collapsed right there in the church. She hasn't come out of her room all morning. The doctor's with her now."

"It wasn't my—"

"Three hundred people," Gerhard interjected. "The mayor was there, for God's sake. And who is this?" Vern's beady black eyes peered in Jackson's direction.

Jackson stepped forward, his sense of justice winning over his instinct for self-preservation. "Do you even want to know what happened?"

"It doesn't take a rocket scientist to figure out what *happened*." Gerhard's attention turned back to Crista. "She got scared. Well, sweetheart, we all get scared. But you don't get scared two minutes before the wedding. You do it the day before, and we talk about it. Or do you do it the day after, and we get a divorce."

Crista's posture sagged. "A divorce?"

Jackson took her elbow, afraid she might go down.

"You'd want a divorce?" she asked Gerhard in a tone of amazement.

"There are ways to do this," he answered. "And this wasn't one of them."

"That's not what happened," said Jackson.

She grasped the hand on her elbow. "Don't."

"Crista didn't get scared," he said. "I'm the one who stopped your wedding."

"Let it go," she whispered. "Don't do it."

He glanced down at her expression. It looked like she'd changed her mind and didn't want him to confess. Well, that worked fine for him.

"Just who are you?" Gerhard demanded again.

"I'm an old boyfriend," he said, crafting a story on the fly. "I showed up at the church. I begged her for another chance. I told her she couldn't marry you until we'd talked."

Vern's jaw went tight. There was anger in his expression, but it didn't exactly look like jealousy. "You ran off with another man?"

"I insisted," said Jackson, bracing for Vern to come at him. If the tables had been turned and Crista had been his bride, Jackson would have taken the man's head off.

Gerhard didn't move. His attention swung back to Crista. "What do you expect me to do?"

"I don't care what you do," she said, determination returning to her tone.

Gerhard took a step forward, and Jackson stepped between them. "Don't touch her."

"Crista, get in the house."

Jackson countered. "Crista, get in the car."

"Mother and Father are owed an explanation," said Gerhard.

"You weren't even interested in her explanation," said Jackson.

"Get out of my way."

"No." Jackson had no intention of leaving Crista behind.

"This is none of your business."

"I'm making it my business."

Gerhard took another step.

Jackson braced his feet apart, willing the guy to take a swing. All he needed was an excuse, and he'd wipe the cocky confidence right off Gerhard's face.

"Please don't hurt him," said Crista.

"Okay," said Jackson.

"She's talking to me," said Gerhard.

Jackson couldn't help but smile at that.

"Please," Crista repeated.

"Get in the car," said Jackson.

"You won't?" she asked.

"I won't," he promised.

"We are not done talking," Gerhard called to Crista.

"Oh, yes, you are." Jackson listened to her footfalls until she slammed the passenger door.

"Make any move, and I'll defend myself," he told Gerhard.

Gerhard didn't look like he was going to try.

Still, Jackson kept an eye over his shoulder as he returned to the vehicle. Half of him hoped Gerhard would come at him. But the smarter half just wanted to get Crista away from this family.

He planted himself behind the wheel.

"Just take me home," she said, yanking her dress into place around her legs.

He started the engine and put the vehicle into gear. "You got it."

They drove away in silence.

It was five minutes before she spoke up. "You know where you're going?"

"I know where you live." He checked his rearview mirror again, making a mental note of vehicles in the block behind them.

"How do you know that?"

"Mac gave me the address."

"Mac, who was investigating Vern."

"Yes."

Both a blue sedan and a silver sports car stayed with them at the left turn.

"This is creepy, you know that?"

"I don't imagine it's any fun," said Jackson.

"You've destroyed my life."

He gave her a quick glance. "You're blaming me?"

"Of course I'm blaming you."

"Because your fiancé's a jerk?"

"Because you ruined my wedding." She paused for a moment. "It's not your fault my fiancé's a jerk."

Jackson almost smiled as he checked the side mirror.

"I don't know what that was all about," she said.

"Maybe he's not the man you thought he was."

"He's never done that before. He's very even tempered, patient, trusting."

"Is this the first time you've seen him under stress?" Jackson was no expert, but he couldn't help but think it was a bad idea to marry someone before you'd had a few knock-down, drag-out fights. A person needed to know who fought dirty and who fought clean.

"Vern's family is important to him," she said.

"You're defending that behavior?"

"He didn't cheat on me."

"He did. But that's not the point. He didn't trust you. He didn't ask you what happened to you. All he cared about was Mommy and Daddy."

Crista didn't seem to have an answer for that.

"We're being tailed," said Jackson.

"What?"

"Tailed. There's a car following us. What does Gerhard drive?"

She twisted her head to look behind them.

"Three back," said Jackson. "The blue Lexus."

"It could be."

"You're not sure?" Who didn't recognize her own boyfriend's car?

"The Gerhards own a lot of cars. I think they have one like that."

"The tribulations of the rich and famous," Jackson drawled.

"Ha-ha."

"What do you want me to do?"

"I sure don't want to talk to him again."

"Good." Jackson was even more concerned than before.

Trent had claimed Gerhard's real interest was a diamond mine. And Gerhard sure hadn't acted like a man afraid for his fiancée's safety. He'd acted like a man with something to lose—maybe money to lose. And now, instead of stewing in his own self-righteousness or giving her a chance to cool down, he was having her followed. This did not strike Jackson as a typical lovers' quarrel.

"Want me to lose the tail?" he asked Crista.

"Can you?"

He smiled to himself. "I can."

"Yes. Do it."

"Seat belt tight?"

"Yes."

"Hang on."

Seeing an intersection coming up, Jackson barged his way across two lanes, moving hard to the left, cutting the yellow way too close and turning onto Crestlake. From there, he took a quick right, drove until they were behind a high-rise and pulled into an underground parking lot.

Crista held on as they bounced over the speed bumps.

He knew the lot had six exits. He took Ray Street, covered three blocks to the park and pulled onto the scenic drive. It would take them over the bridge to the interstate. After that, they could get as far away as she wanted.

"Did we lose him?" she asked, stretching to look out the rear window.

"We lost him."

They'd probably lost him at the underground, but Jackson had wanted to be certain.

She tugged at the stiff neckline of her dress in obvious frustration, pulling it away from her cleavage. "I need some time to think."

She looked tired and uncomfortable.

"Is there somewhere you want to go?"

"Not to my place, that's for sure."

"You could probably use a change of clothes."

She tugged at the fabric again. "I'm getting a rash."

"We'll take the next exit, find someplace to buy you a pair of blue jeans."

"That would be a relief. I'd also like to throw this thing in a Dumpster."

Jackson liked that idea very much. "I can make that happen."

"Thanks."

"No problem."

"I mean, really. Thanks, Jackson. You didn't have to do any of this."

He shrugged. "I fix problems. You have a problem."

"You don't even know me."

He felt like he did know her, at least a little bit. And

what he knew he admired. "I don't have to know you to help you."

"Most people don't think like that."

"Lucky for you, you ran into me."

Her brows rose in skepticism. "Ran into you?"

"I see an exit." He didn't want to get into any of the details of his investigation. He sure didn't want her asking again about who'd sent him.

She watched out the side window. "Looks like a shopping mall down there."

"That'll do. You want to go in and try things on or just tell me your size?"

She looked down at the billow of her skirt. "I'll wait in the car, if you don't mind."

"Worried you might attract attention?"

"The last thing I need is for someone to snap a picture and post it to social media."

He nodded in approval. He was relieved she understood she was being chased by the Gerhards. "Good call. I can see you going viral in that outfit."

She heaved a deep sigh, her cleavage catching his attention so that he nearly swerved off the exit ramp.

"I was supposed to be on a yacht today," she said. "Bobbing around the Mediterranean, sipping chardonnay, reading a celebrity magazine and working on my tan."

Mentally, Jackson added that she would have been under Gerhard's control, at the mercy of his family. His suspicions were pinging in earnest. Gerhard wasn't a worried groom. He was a thwarted con artist.

If everything Trent said was true, the Gerhards were organized and ruthless, and they sure wouldn't want to lose track of Crista. She'd been gone for twenty-four hours. There was every chance Daddy Gerhard had people on her apartment by now. They might even be watching her credit cards and bank account.

Jackson was definitely looking into the diamond mine, its size and location, its ownership, and how it could possibly have made it onto Gerhard's radar.

Crista was going to pay Jackson back for everything just as soon as she had access to her bank account.

For now, explaining that he was invoking his regular precautions, he'd put her up at the Fountain Lake Family Hotel, leaving his own credit card information with the front desk to cover her expenses. The place was full of boisterous vacationers, and it seemed like an easy place for her to blend in with the crowd. Her room was spacious, with a king-size bed, comfy sitting area, a small kitchenette and a furnished balcony overlooking the pool and a minigolf course.

She'd tried right away to call Ellie, her best friend and maid of honor, but she only got through to voice mail. It seemed far too complicated to leave a message, so she'd decided to try again later. Instead, she liberated a soft drink from the minibar and wandered onto the balcony.

The temperature was in the high eighties, but a breeze was blowing across the lake, cooling the air. She was on the third floor, so it was easy to make out the activity below, kids splashing in the pool, teenagers lounging on striped towels. There was a young couple in one of the gazebos. He was slathering suntan lotion on her bare back, playfully untying her bathing suit top.

The woman batted awkwardly at his hand to get him to stop. When he kissed the back of her neck and looped his arms around her, Crista quickly looked away. They were probably on their honeymoon.

She eased onto a rattan lounger, wishing she had a bathing suit herself. She wondered if Jackson's credit card was connected to the hotel shops as well as the restaurants. It would definitely be nice to take a swim, and since her three jewelry stores, Cristal Creations, were doing very well, it would be a simple matter to pay back every dime.

Afterward, she'd order something from the room service menu. She'd get a bottle of wine. Maybe gaze at the moon and the stars out here and get some perspective on life. She toyed with her engagement ring, twisting it around and around as she went over the confrontation with Vern.

He'd been quick to assume she'd run away. She was disappointed, of course, but she wasn't sure she could blame him completely for his reaction. It must have seemed like the most logical conclusion at the time. Though it would have been nice if he'd asked her what happened.

The worst part was that he'd suggested divorce. As if getting married and then quickly divorcing was preferable to ruining a party. He'd worried about the embarrassment to his family. He'd worried about her dress, his mother and the mayor. The only thing he didn't seem to worry about was Crista.

In the thick of the argument, it had seemed clear that it was over. But now other memories were crowding in, good memories. Did one ugly argument obliterate everything they'd shared?

On the other hand, it had been an alarming experience, seeing a side of Vern she'd never known existed. She found herself questioning the photographs, no longer completely convinced they were fake.

She took another swig of the soda. Maybe she should

call him. Or maybe she should confront him in person again, flat-out ask him if he was cheating.

Maybe he'd tell her the truth. Or maybe he wouldn't. Or maybe she'd never know.

She came to her feet.

Ellie was her next phone call, not Vern. Ellie would have good advice. She always did.

Crista pulled open the glass door, entering the cool of the air-conditioned room. She was chilled for a moment, but then it felt good. She sat down on the bed and dialed nine for an outside line. Then she punched in Ellie's number.

Before the line connected, there was a knock on the door.

Crista didn't need towels or mints or anything else from a housekeeper. But she also didn't want a hotel employee barging in on her conversation. She quickly replaced the telephone receiver and went to the peephole.

It was Jackson.

Puzzled, she drew open the door. "Did you forget something?"

"Yes." He walked in without an invitation.

"Come on in," she muttered, letting the door swing shut behind him.

"I forget to tell you not to phone anyone from the room."

"Not even Ellie?"

"Who's Ellie?"

"My maid of honor."

"Not even Ellie. The Gerhards have a big security staff. They'll be covering all the angles."

"Their security staff looks after the Gerhard buildings. They don't care about Vern's love life."

"They care about what Manfred Gerhard tells them to care about."

"You're paranoid. And anyway, I thought you'd left."

"I'm not in a hurry."

"You don't have a job to get back to? A life that requires your attention?"

Instead of answering, he sat himself down on the small blue sofa. "What do you know about the Borezone Mine?"

"What's the Borezone Mine?"

"Have you ever heard of it?"

"No. Was it in the news?"

"No."

She waited for him to elaborate, but he didn't. She wondered if he was making small talk, delaying his departure for some reason. She tried to figure out why he might want to hang around.

"I won't go wild with your credit card, if that's what's got you worried," she tried.

"I'm not worried about my credit card."

"Are you worried I'll make a phone call? Because it won't matter if I do."

"Ha. Now I'm definitely worried you'll make a phone call."

"I need to talk to Ellie." What she needed was a girlfriend to listen to her fears about Vern.

"Talk to me instead."

She took the armchair cornerwise from where he sat. "Sure. I'll just sit here and bare my soul to the strange man who kidnapped me from my wedding. I can't see any downside to that."

"Good. Go ahead. Bare away."

"You're not funny."

Surely he could understand that this was traumatic for her.

"You absolutely need to call Ellie?" he asked.

"Yes."

With a shake of his head and an expression that looked like disgust, he pulled out his phone. But instead of handing it over, he dialed a number.

"What's Ellie's last name?"

"Sharpley. Why?"

"It's me," he said into the phone. "Crista needs to make a call. Ellie Sharpley." He paused, sliding an exasperated glance her way. "I know. It's a girl thing."

Crista squared her shoulders. "A girl thing?"

"Let me know when it's done."

"A *girl* thing?" she repeated.

He pocketed his phone. "What would you call it?"

"A conversation. A human thing."

"You'll be able to have one in about an hour. Are you hungry? You must be hungry."

"You must have people you talk things over with. Friends? Relationships?"

"I'm pretty independent."

"No girlfriend?" For some reason, she'd assumed he was single. But there was no reason for that assumption. Well, other than the way he'd kissed her. But he had only kissed her.

"No girlfriend," he said.

She was relieved. No, she wasn't relieved. She didn't care. His love life was nothing to her.

"Hungry?" he repeated.

She was hungry. She'd barely eaten yesterday. She'd been watching calories for weeks now, wanting a svelte silhouette in the formfitting dress. In retrospect, her waist size was the least of her worries. But now there wasn't a reason in the world not to indulge in pizza or pasta, or maybe some chocolate cake.

"I'm starving," she said. "I know it's only lunchtime, but any chance we can get a martini?"

"There's a patio café overlooking the back nine."

"Sold."

A martini wouldn't help her make a better decision, but it would relax her in the short term. Relaxed was good. She could use some relaxing.

She came to her feet. "It feels strange not to take a purse."

He rose with her, and they made their way toward the door. "You want to buy a purse?"

"I've got nothing to put in it."

"We could buy you a comb or some lipstick or something."

She couldn't help but appreciate his offer. She also couldn't help wondering about his motivation. It was strange that he was still here, stranger still that he was putting out an effort to help her.

She exited into the hallway. "Are you feeling guilty?"

He checked to see that the door had locked behind them, then fell into step beside her. "For what?"

"For destroying my life."

"Gerhard was the one trying to destroy your life."

"Jury's still out on that."

Sure, Vern had been a jerk back at the mansion. But to be fair, he'd been under stress. She could only imagine his parents' reaction to the disappearance of the bride. Poor Vern had been alone with them, bearing the brunt of their displeasure for nearly twenty-four hours.

Jackson pressed the elevator button. "The pictures are real, Crista."

"Can you prove it?"

"I'm sure we can. Let me look into the options for that."

They stepped onto the elevator, and it descended.

"We've been together for nearly a year," she said.

It wasn't a whirlwind. And it sure didn't make sense for Vern to marry her if he was involved with someone else.

"People aren't always honest, Crista."

She found herself glancing up at his expression. "Are you honest?"

He met her gaze. "I try to be."

"Well, there's a nonanswer."

"In my profession, I can't always tell everybody everything."

"So you only lie professionally."

There was a trace of amusement in his tone. "Not personally, and not recreationally."

"Interesting moral framework."

The doors slid open.

She started to move, but Jackson's hand shot out to block her, coming to rest on her stomach.

"What?"

He pulled her to one side then stabbed his finger hard on the close door button.

"What are you doing?"

The doors slid shut.

"You must have talked to someone since we've been here."

"No. Well, I tried to phone Ellie. But I got her voice mail. I didn't even leave a message."

Jackson swore as he punched twelve, the top floor.

"What?"

"Vern. He's in the lobby with a couple of guys."

"No way."

"I just saw him."

The elevator rose.

"How is that possible?"

"It's possible because your phone call connected and revealed the hotel number."

"I didn't call Vern." Wasn't Jackson listening? "I called Ellie."

"And Vern knows Ellie's number. They were monitoring her phone."

"That's ridiculous."

"You have a better explanation for him showing up here?"

She didn't. In fact, she was baffled. And she was starting to feel frightened.

"What do we do on the twelfth floor?" she asked as the numbers pinged higher.

"My room," he said.

It seemed every second threw her for another loop. "You have a room? Why would you need a room?"

"To sleep in. You can have a drink there."

"But why would you sleep here?"

"So I can drive you back to the city when you're ready."

"I thought I was going to take a bus back to the city."

"If we'd gone with that plan, Gerhard would already have you."

"Jackson, *what* is going on?"

It took him a moment to answer. He seemed to be weighing his words. "Vern Gerhard wants you back, and he has a lot of money to spend accomplishing that."

"I *was* coming back." She thought about that statement. "I mean, I might go back. I didn't break up with him. I still have his ring."

The doors opened on twelve.

"You should break up with him." Jackson gestured for her to exit first. "Take a right."

"I don't know for sure that he's done anything wrong. Well, except react badly to me wrecking a hundred-thousand-dollar wedding."

"You didn't wreck it."

"You did."

"True enough," he said.

He inserted a key card into a set of double doors at the end of the hallway.

"You don't seem to care."

"I don't care about Gerhard's money, that's for sure."

Crista stepped over the threshold, taken aback by the very well-appointed suite. She gazed around. "Used to traveling in style?"

"I thought I might need a room for a meeting."

"With me?" They needed a meeting?

"With Mac and some of the other guys. They'll be here later."

She digested that statement. "There's something you're not telling me."

"There are hundreds of things I'm not telling you."

The door swung shut behind him and he crossed to a wet bar.

"Those pictures of Vern are fake, aren't they? Is this extortion? Am I still kidnapped? Was this about money all along?"

"We have beer, wine or highballs. And I'm going to order room service. If you're set on a martini, I can have them bring one."

"That's not an answer."

It occurred to her that she might be a whole lot safer with Vern. The suite door was right behind her. She could be out of it before Jackson caught her. Could she make it to the elevator, or would he drag her back kicking and screaming?

"You're not kidnapped," he told her, exasperation clear in his tone. "I left you alone in your room for an hour."

She eased a bit closer to the double doors. "You could have been standing guard outside my door."

"I wasn't. I'm a whole lot more interested in food right now that I am in any of Gerhard's moves. You're free to leave. You've been free to leave since this morning. I took you back to their mansion. You could have stayed there."

He was right about that. She could have walked inside the mansion where the Gerhard family, not to mention a few security guards who would have been waiting. There wouldn't have been a thing Jackson could do to stop her.

She wasn't being held against her will.

"I'll take a glass of merlot," she told him. "And I'd kill for a mushroom and sausage pizza."

He smiled at that. "Coming up."

"We told Vern your name this morning," she felt compelled to point out. "He can probably find your room number."

"What makes you think I'm registered under my own name?" He uncorked a bottle of wine and gestured to a living room furniture grouping. "Probably better to stay off the patio."

"You've got me worried there's a sniper out there," she joked.

He crossed the room with two glasses of wine, setting them on opposite ends of a coffee table. "I'd say a long lens rather than a rifle. But it's healthy to be cautious."

"Of the whole family now?" She took one end of the sofa and lifted her wine.

"The whole family," said Jackson, giving her a mock toast.

She drank, anticipating the hit of alcohol and glad of it. These had been the strangest days of her life. She wished the insanity was over, but it seemed there was more to come.

Five

To Jackson's surprise, Mac wasn't alone.

There was a twentysomething woman in the hotel hallway beside him. She had short, dark hair, blue eyes, a pert nose and set of distracting, full red lips.

In five years working together, Jackson had never seen his security agent behave so unprofessionally. "You brought a *date*?"

"I'm not his date," the woman stated with a sniff of disgust.

"Ellie?" Crista called out from behind him.

"She's not my date," said Mac.

Ellie pushed past Jackson.

"She's the maid of honor," said Mac.

"And you brought her *here*?" Jackson wasn't sure if that made it better or worse.

The two women laughed and embraced.

"I've been frantic," said Ellie, her voice high. "We thought you were hurt or dead."

"She was frantic." Mac's tone was dry as he shut the door behind himself.

"Did anybody see you two come in?" asked Jackson, wondering if Mac had lost his mind. "Gerhard is definitely going to recognize the maid of honor."

"I saw him down there," said Mac. "And I saw his guys. They didn't see us."

"You're positive?"

"I'm positive."

Jackson felt a bit better.

"It's been crazy," said Crista, pulling Ellie toward the sofa. "Jackson hauled me away from the church. Then we were on a boat. I jumped off. When I finally got home, Vern was an absolute jerk about it."

"That doesn't sound like Vern."

"I *know*. He's acting weird. I'm so confused about this whole thing. But tell me what happened after I left."

As Ellie began to talk, Jackson returned his attention to Mac. "I thought you were giving her a burner phone."

"That was my plan."

"Didn't work out for you?"

Hearing Ellie's earnest tone and the pace of her speech, Jackson thought he could understand why.

"Not so much," said Mac.

"Talked you into the ground."

"Something like that."

"Drink?" asked Jackson.

"A beer if you've got it."

The two men moved to the wet bar, and Mac perched himself on one of the stools.

Jackson lowered his voice, glancing to the sofa where Crista and Ellie were engrossed in conversation. "I'm buying Trent's story now. This isn't just about a runaway bride."

Mac nodded. "Those guys in the lobby look way too serious for that."

Jackson twisted the tops off two bottles of beer. "We need to look into the diamond mine."

"Norway's already on it."

Jackson was glad to hear that. "Anything jumping out at him?"

"The Borezone Mine has been around forever. Trent Corday originally bought it twenty years ago at a bargain price. He nearly lost it for noncompliance with the claim. Then he did lose a huge chunk of it, apparently on a gambling debt."

"To who?"

"That's not exactly clear. Shell companies are hiding behind holding companies. But we've confirmed he put his remaining shares in his daughter's name."

"A moment of mental clarity?" Jackson speculated, thinking it was possible Trent recognized his own incompetence with money.

"Or a moment of making amends. It sounds like he was in and out of her life over the years, never provided much in the way of monetary or any other kind of support. He wasn't exactly father of the year. On the other hand, the mine wasn't worth much at the time."

"And now?"

Trent had said there'd been a recent discovery, but that could mean a lot of things.

"Depends on who you talk to," said Mac. "A numbered Cayman Islands company currently owns the majority. We haven't been able to trace the principals behind it, but they hired an exploration company that made the latest discovery. They're hyping it as a hundred million resource, talking about going public with a share offering."

"Could all be a scam—pump the share price and dump the stock on unsuspecting investors."

"Most likely," said Mac. "But we'll keep looking."

Jackson tipped back his beer and took a drink. For Crista's sake, he hoped it was a scam. The last thing she needed was a multimillion-dollar stake in a diamond mine and a group of shady characters out to exploit her.

"Is that how Gerhard found out?" he asked. "Through the exploration company's hype?"

Mac frowned. "That's the strange part. The timing doesn't add up. The hype started six months ago. Gerhard's been with Crista for a year."

"So he found out some other way."

"Or the wedding had nothing to do with the diamond mine."

"I don't believe that for a second," said Jackson. "Those guys in the lobby tell me there's lots of money at stake."

Mac nodded. Jackson's attention switched to Crista. Vern Gerhard had targeted her for the money. Jackson was certain of it. But nothing pointed to how Gerhard found out about the mine. Jackson was missing a piece, maybe more than one. There was definitely something he didn't know, and it seemed likely it was something that could hurt Crista.

"What's next?" asked Mac.

"Norway stays on the mine." Jackson formulated an initial plan in his mind. "You take Gerhard—especially look for any link between his family and that Cayman Islands company. I'll take another look at Trent. There might be more to this story than he's let on."

"Can do," said Mac. "One question."

"What's that?"

"Has someone actually hired us for this job? I mean, besides the two convicts making eight dollars a day?"

"I can't do a favor for my father?" Jackson acknowledged that things had gone beyond the few hours of time he'd planned to spend looking into Gerhard.

"You can, but you don't." Mac looked pointedly at Crista who was smiling at Ellie. "If she wasn't a bona fide ten, would you be dedicating so many resources for free?"

"We'll never know," said Jackson. "She's not going to stop being a ten, and my curiosity's going now."

"Lots of pretty women in the world."

Jackson saw Mac's gaze shift from Crista to Ellie.

"Not a lot of diamond mines."

Mac snorted a laugh. "You don't care about a diamond mine."

"True." But Jackson was finding that he did care about Crista.

It didn't make sense, but he did care. Sure, she was beautiful. And she was in some kind of trouble. And Gerhard didn't deserve to be within a mile of her. But something else was drawing him in.

The closest he could come was that her circumstances were similar to his. She'd lost her mother as a young adult, and her father was in prison. It might be as simple as that. They were kindred spirits. She wasn't as tough as him. She wasn't as capable of taking care of herself, and he was offended that the Gerhards had targeted her.

Ellie suddenly twisted and spoke up. "Any danger in ordering room service?"

Jackson was reminded that he and Crista were practically starving.

"None at all," he said, straightening away from the bar.

"I was all set for pizza," said Crista, seeming rather cheerful under the circumstances.

"I'm in," said Ellie.

"And chocolate cake," said Crista. "Do you think they'd have chocolate cake?"

Jackson moved to the phone on a side table. "I'll ask."

"It's not like I have to fit into that dress anymore," Crista said to Ellie.

"You can always get something a size bigger," Ellie returned on a laugh.

"I'm not going to eat that much cake."

Jackson paused with the phone in his hand, not liking where she seemed to be going.

"What do you mean?" he asked Crista.

"I mean one piece will be enough."

"I'll take one, too," said Ellie.

"Get a round," said Mac.

"You're talking about getting another wedding dress," Jackson said. "Why would you need another wedding dress?"

Crista looked back at him. "The last one got ruined, remember?"

Both Ellie and Mac disappeared from his vision as it tunneled to Crista. "But you're not getting married anymore."

"Maybe not."

"Maybe?"

"I know he was a jerk back there. But it was a stressful situation. He had to cope with his parents and all those dignitaries. It had to be incredibly embarrassing."

Jackson took a step toward her, hardly able to believe her words. "You're defending him?"

"It wasn't his finest moment, but—"

"He's messing around on you. He's *been* messing around on you for months."

"We don't know that."

Jackson jabbed his thumb in Mac's direction. "Mac is completely trustworthy."

"I don't know Mac. I never met Mac until today."

"I know Mac."

"Well, *I* don't know you."

"You'd actually give that jerk a second chance?" Did Jackson need to rethink his involvement in all this?

"We can validate the photos," said Mac.

"Why should we do that?" Jackson demanded, annoyance getting the better of him.

"To give Crista peace of mind."

"She doesn't want to believe us, that's her problem. In fact, she can head down to the lobby right now if she thinks Gerhard is so trustworthy."

"Hang on." Ellie came to her feet. "I'm not a Vern fan. But I'd be—"

"What do you mean, you're not a Vern fan?" Crista sat up straight, obviously shocked by the statement.

Ellie seemed to realize what she'd said. Her expression turned guilty.

"Explain," said Crista. "You said you liked him."

"I do. Well, you know, sort of."

"Sort of?"

"There are things about him that I like."

Jackson eased back, waiting to see where the conversation would lead. He was relieved by Ellie's support.

"He's always generous," said Ellie. "And he's always happy."

Jackson couldn't help thinking she hadn't seen his behavior this morning.

"Maybe too happy," she continued. "It's a bit unnatural, don't you think?"

"You're criticizing him for being happy?" Crista was clearly confused by Ellie's attitude.

"There's something about him that's too polished," said Ellie. "My radar sometimes kicks in. Like, he's saying and doing all the right things, but the sincerity's not there in his eyes."

Jackson was beginning to like Ellie.

Crista came to her feet. "Why didn't you say something before now?"

"You seemed so happy," said Ellie in an apologetic tone. "I wanted it to all be true. But now…"

"You've changed your mind because of some pictures? Pictures obtained by a stranger who is obviously willing to break the law, and who has something, some scheme, going on that we don't understand."

"A scheme?" Now Jackson was offended.

Mac stepped in. "I think I'll go ahead and order. Pizza and chocolate cake?"

"All I'm saying," Ellie said, gesturing with both hands as if she was appealing for calm, "is why not verify the photos? What could it hurt?"

Crista didn't seem to have an answer for that.

Quite frankly, neither did Jackson. He knew the photos were authentic. And once Crista knew it, too, she'd start to trust him. He realized he wanted that. He wanted it too much for comfort.

That wasn't good. It wasn't good at all. His instincts with her could lead him into all sorts of trouble.

* * *

Crista savored a final bite of the moist chocolate cake decorated with decadent swirls of buttercream icing.

"I bet this was better than the wedding cake," said Ellie, licking her fork.

The two women had moved outside onto the hotel suite balcony. Now that darkness had fallen, Jackson deemed it safe to sit there. He'd pointed out that someone with night-vision binoculars in a neighboring building might still be able to make them out. But he'd admitted the likelihood of that was low.

"I wonder what they did with the wedding cake," Crista mused.

"Not to mention the crab puffs. And what about the ice sculpture?"

"I suppose they could keep it in the freezer."

"For the next wedding with a precious gems theme?"

"It was unique." Crista thought back to the geometric base and the embedded colored stones.

"I thought Mrs. Gerhard was going to have an aneurysm," said Ellie. "She turned all kinds of mottled red. Manfred was bellowing orders. Security guards were rushing all over the building, out on the sidewalk. Man, I wish I'd had my cell phone to take some video."

"Have you checked social media?" Crista hated to think it, but it seemed likely somebody had taken pictures. Vern would be mortified at having the world believe he was left at the altar.

"It'll be all over town by now," said Ellie. "The bachelorettes of Chicago will either be laughing at him or hauling out their push-up bras."

Having been with Vern for a year, Crista knew how many women out there were vying for his attention. He'd been devoted to Crista, but it was clear his ego appreciated the attention from others. He'd hate the thought of becoming a joke.

A clanging sound suddenly blasted through the air.

Both women jumped up, clasping their hands over their ears.

"What on earth?" asked Ellie.

Jackson immediately bolted through the balcony doorway. He grasped Crista and pulled her back into the suite. Mac was there, too, ushering Ellie inside.

"It's the fire alarm," said Jackson.

"Gerhard," said Mac.

"Trying to flush us out."

"He wouldn't do that," said Crista.

Vern was restrained and circumspect, not to mention law-abiding. He'd never pull a false fire alarm.

"He did do that," Jackson said with conviction. "And we're not going anywhere."

"You can't know it was him," she protested.

Sirens sounded in the distance.

"There are at least six fire exits in the building," said Mac.

Jackson was glancing around. "He must have brought in more men to watch them all."

"This is ridiculous," said Crista.

Jackson and Mac exchanged some kind of a knowing look.

"Uh, guys," Ellie broke in as she gaped through the open balcony door. "I see smoke out there."

That got everybody's attention. Crista wrinkled her nose, realizing she could smell it, too.

Ellie pointed. "That's definitely smoke."

Mac was outside like a shot.

"Flames," he called over his shoulder. "Fifth floor."

He came back inside. "And the third floor in the other wing."

"He set two fires?" Jackson asked, half to himself.

"What now?" asked Mac.

"We *leave the building*," said Crista. Like there was any question about it.

"You take Ellie," said Jackson. "Leave through the back."

"Will do," said Mac.

"Crista and I will go through the lobby. It'll be easier to hide in the crowd than anything else."

"Good luck," said Mac. He looked to Ellie. "Let's go."

She grabbed her purse from the coffee table and gave Crista a quick hug. "I'll call you."

Crista felt like she'd been swept up in someone else's life. "Vern didn't light the building on fire."

"I hope not," said Ellie, pulling away. But her expression said she thought it was possible.

"But—" Before Crista could finish the sentence, Ellie was out the suite door with Mac.

Jackson grabbed two hand towels and doused them with water. Then he handed her one.

"Hold this over your face and cough. Pretend the smoke is bothering you."

"This is crazy."

Jackson put a hand on her back and propelled her toward the door. "He's determined."

"I was going to call him tomorrow."

"I guess he didn't want to wait."

"This is a coincidence."

"It doesn't matter," said Jackson.

"Of course it matters. You've accused my fiancé of arson." She fell silent as they left the suite.

There were other people in the hall, some quiet, some speculating about the smell of smoke, all making their way toward the staircase.

"You might want to start referring to him as your ex-fiancé," Jackson said in her ear.

"I'm still wearing his ring."

"You can take it off anytime."

He reached over her head to grab the top of the door, holding it open as she walked through then handing it off to the man behind him.

"Protocol says I have to give it back to him," said Crista as they started down.

"So, you *are* giving it back."

"I don't know. I don't know what to do. I don't even know what to think. Do I have to answer this very moment?"

"No. You just have to stick with me. And quit defending him. And put the towel over your face. We're almost there."

The lobby door was held open by successive people exiting. When they cleared the stairwell, Jackson pulled her close beside him.

"See that family?" He pointed to a man, woman and three kids out front of them.

"Yes."

"Go walk with them. Talk to the wife if you can. Gerhard's looking for a couple, so you want to pretend you're with them."

Crista had to admit, it made sense. At least it made as much sense as anything else that was going on today.

"Okay," she agreed.

"Don't look for me. I'll keep you in sight. Just go where they go, and I'll meet you outside."

She nodded.

"Now cough."

She coughed, and he gave her a little shove of encouragement. She quickened her pace and came up beside the woman who was holding the hand of the young girl.

"Did you smell the smoke?" Crista asked her.

"We were on the fifth floor," said the woman, looking stricken. "The fire was right down the hall. We had to leave everything behind."

"Bunny," said the little girl, tears in her eyes.

"Bunny will be fine," the woman whispered, voice breaking.

Crista's heart went out to the frightened girl, and she gave her a squeeze on the shoulder. "The firemen are here. They'll use their hoses to put the fire out."

A dozen firefighters in helmets and gold-colored coveralls strode across the crowded lobby.

"Will Bunny get wet?" asked the girl.

"Bunny might get wet," said Crista. "But it'll be like a bath. Is Bunny a boy or a girl?"

"A girl."

"Does she like baths?"

"I dunno."

"Do you like baths?"

The girl nodded. "Uh-huh. I get bubbles and baby froggy. He hops on the water and spits out his mouth."

"Thank you," the woman whispered in Crista's ear, obviously grateful for the distraction.

They'd come to the front doors, which were wide-open, the night air blowing inside. The drive was a maze of fire trucks, ambulances and police vehicles. Lights flashed and uniformed people rushed past. Some were on radios, some hauling hoses and other gear, and some were aiding people to stretchers or ambulances.

The hotel guests had obviously come out of the building in whatever they were wearing. Few had sweaters, many were barefoot. They looked confused and disoriented.

For a moment, Crista could only stand and stare.

She suddenly felt an arm go firmly around her shoulders. She glanced up, afraid it was Vern. But it was Jackson.

"Let's go," he said, moving her forward.

"This is awful."

"It's under control."

"He didn't do this. He couldn't have done this." The fire had to be an accident.

"I'm not going to argue with you," said Jackson, increasing their pace around the end of a fire truck.

"You don't believe me."

"That's the least of our worries. We need to get out of here. We'll never get my car from the valet, but there's a rental place a couple of blocks away."

"I should just talk to him." The sooner she got it over with, the better.

"No, you shouldn't." Taking her hand, Jackson set an angled course across the front lawn.

She had to struggle to keep up to his pace. "I'll have to talk to him eventually."

"You can phone him."

"I thought I wasn't allowed to phone anyone."

"Don't twist my words."

She came to a halt, yanking her hand from his, annoyed by his high-handed attitude. This was still her life.

"I'm not twisting your words."

He stopped, let his shoulders drop and turned back.

"You'll be able to call him, just not tonight, and not on a phone with a GPS."

"I really don't mind talking to him."

She wasn't excited about it. But the prospect of a conversation didn't need to get blown all out of proportion, either. She'd sit Vern down, look him in the eyes and tell him...

She realized she didn't exactly know what she'd tell him. Would she hand him back the ring and break it off completely? Would she ask for an explanation of his behavior? Would she demand to know if he'd been faithful?

"Crista?" Jackson interrupted.

She looked up.

"You need to sleep on this."

She recognized that he was right. That had been her first instinct. She should get a good night's sleep. It would all be clearer in the morning.

She nodded her agreement and started to walk.

To her surprise, he took her hand again. But this time his touch was gentle, and he slowed his pace.

She knew she shouldn't be grateful. He was her kidnapper, not her friend, and there were all kinds of reasons she shouldn't trust him. But she found she did trust him. And at the moment, there was no denying that she also felt gratitude.

"Thank you," she said.

He glanced down as they walked. "For what this time?"

"Rescuing me from a burning building, I guess."

He grinned at that. "Sure. No problem. I had to follow you down quite a few stairs, but that's the kind of guy I am."

"What kind?" she asked, her curiosity piqued.

"What kind what?"

"What kind of guy are you? Tell me. What would you be doing right now if you weren't with me?"

"Probably working another case."

"At ten o'clock on a Sunday night?"

"Mine isn't a nine-to-five job."

She supposed it wasn't. He'd already said he didn't have a girlfriend. "What about family and friends?"

"No family. Friends, sure. But there's not a lot of time in my life for anything serious."

"When was your last girlfriend?"

"It's been a while."

She waited, but he didn't elaborate.

"You know all about my love life," she said.

"That's a professional interest."

"Well, fair's fair. Spill."

"You see that sign?" He pointed down the street.

"The car rental place?" The familiar sign flashed orange and white on the next corner.

"That's where we're going."

"Don't think you can change the subject that easily."

"It was two years ago," he said, increasing their pace. "Her name was Melanie. She's an accountant."

In Crista's mind, it didn't fit. "You dated an accountant?"

"Something wrong with that?"

"Are you making that up?"

"Why would I make it up? You don't think I can get dates?"

The suggestion was preposterous. Jackson was a smart, successful, sexy guy. He could get all the dates he wanted.

"An accountant doesn't sound very exciting," she

said as they hustled across a side street to the rental car parking lot.

"Maybe I wasn't looking for exciting."

"Jackson, everything about you says you're looking for exciting."

"How so?"

"Take this weekend. You kidnapped a bride, told one of Chicago's wealthiest men to stuff it, and there's a hotel on fire behind you."

"That doesn't mean I like it." He pulled open the glass door.

"You love it." She grinned over her shoulder as she walked past him and into the small lobby.

There was a single clerk at the counter who was already helping another customer. Crista entered the roped lineup area and followed the pattern to the front, where she stopped to wait.

Jackson came up behind her.

"See that sign on the wall?" he mumbled in her ear. "Behind the counter, with the purple letters."

"That says Weekly Rates?"

"That's the one. Do not turn your head. But look at the reflection in it."

She squinted, seeing a slightly distorted black SUV.

"That's Vern," said Jackson.

She started to look behind her.

"Don't turn," he reminded her sharply.

She held still. "Are you sure?"

"Absolutely. I want you to turn and look at me. Do *not* glance out the front window. Just ask me a question."

She turned. "What question."

"Any question."

"Tell me some more about Melanie the accountant."

"Maybe later. See that hallway at the end of the counter?" He pointed.

She looked. "Yes."

"There's a ladies' room down there. I want you to walk down the hall, go past the ladies' room and out the back door. You can cut through the alley to Greenway. Hail a cab on Greenway. I'll be out in a minute."

"We're not renting a car?"

"We're not renting a car."

"If I talk to him, it'll stop all this madness."

Before she could move, Jackson blocked her way. "It's not safe."

"I'm going to tell him to back off and that we can have a proper conversation tomorrow. He didn't light any hotel on fire."

"If the fire wasn't a ruse to flush you out, why was he waiting to follow us?"

She opened her mouth. But then she realized it was a reasonable question. Vern had to have been outside in the SUV in order to find her.

"It could have been a coincidence," she ventured. It was possible he just happened to see them leaving the hotel.

"Could have been," said Jackson, surprising her with his lack of argument.

It seemed he'd finally decided to leave it up to her. He was letting her assess the situation and make up her own mind. It was heartening but somehow unsettling.

For some reason, without Jackson's pressure, she found herself looking at both sides. She thought her way through each scenario and decided to play it safe.

"Down the hallway?" she confirmed. "Hail a cab?"

"Good decision. I'll be right behind you."

She resisted the urge to look closer at the SUV. Instead, she sauntered toward the hallway, trying to look like she was visiting the ladies' room. She didn't know how to transmit that message by the way she walked, but she did her best.

As Jackson had said, there was an exit door out the back. It led to a small parking area surrounded on two sides by a cinder-block wall. There was a Dumpster in the corner, and several vehicles in various states of disrepair.

She walked cautiously across the uneven pavement, coming to an alleyway where she could see a driveway between two buildings that presumably led to Greenway Street. Avoiding the puddles, she hurried down the dark driveway to the lights of the busy street.

It took a few minutes to catch a cab. By then Jackson had appeared, sliding into the seat beside her.

"Anthony's Bar and Grill at Baffin and Pine."

"We're going for a drink?" she asked, surprised he'd suggest something so mundane, though not really knowing what to expect.

"I'm thirsty, aren't you?" he asked.

She wasn't yet ready to brush past their cloak-and-dagger escape. "How did you know there was a back entrance to the rental place? And how did you know where it would lead?"

"I didn't pick the Fountain Lake Hotel by accident."

"You've been here before," she said, glancing back while the taxi pulled away from the curb, comprehension dawning. "You've done this before."

"I've eluded a few people in the past." His easy smile told her he knew what he was doing. He actually seemed to be enjoying himself.

"You think this is fun." She'd meant it to sound like

an accusation, but it didn't. Truth was, she found his confidence reassuring.

"I think you're fun."

"I'm not having fun. My life is falling apart around my ears, so I am not having any fun at all."

"You'll like Anthony's," he said.

What she'd like was her life back. And she almost said so. But just as quickly she realized it wasn't true. She had no life to get back, at least not a real life, not an honest life. There was nowhere for her to go but forward.

"I'd like a strong drink," she said instead.

"Coming up," said Jackson as the taxi picked up speed.

"This is the strangest day of my life," she muttered.

"I wouldn't trade mine for the world." His tone was unmistakably intimate, bringing with it a wave of desire that heated her chest.

She wanted to look at him, meet his warm eyes, drink in his tender smile. But she didn't dare. No matter what Vern had said or done, she had no right to feel this way about Jackson.

She fixed her gaze on the traffic, bright headlights whizzing past in a rush. She didn't know Jackson. She didn't like Jackson. By this time tomorrow, he'd be nothing but a fading memory.

Six

Despite the humble name, Jackson knew Anthony's was an upscale restaurant housed in a redbrick colonial mansion. Owned by a close friend of his, its high ceilings, ornate woodwork and sweeping staircase gave an ambience of grandeur and a distinct sensation of class.

Tonight, he hadn't been interested in the restaurant, but in the historic B and B rooms on the third floor of the building. He knew he could count on Anthony not to ask questions or keep a record of their stay. It was the closest thing Jackson had to a safe house.

Their room had a four-poster king-size bed, a stone fireplace and sloped cedarwood ceilings. There was a small dining table in a bay window alcove, and a sofa that the housekeeper had already converted into a second bed.

Crista had opted to take a shower, while Jackson had stretched out on top of the sofa bed, a news station playing on the television and his laptop open to the photos of Vern and Gracie. The resolution on the pictures was high, so it was going to be easy to show they hadn't been altered.

His browsing was interrupted when the bathroom door opened and Crista appeared. She was dressed in a fluffy white robe, drying her auburn hair with a towel.

"That shouldn't be all it takes to make me feel better," she said in a cheerful voice as she padded toward him on bare feet. "But it does." She plunked down on the opposite side of the sofa. "I'm refreshed."

Just her appearance made him feel better. She was easy on the eyes and entertaining for his mind. He realized the only thing he liked better than looking at her was listening to her.

"I don't know if this will make you feel better or worse." It certainly made him feel better.

He slid the laptop across the sofa bed toward her. "I've zoomed way in on the pixels. Stare all you want. The pictures haven't been altered."

She shifted on the bed and moved the computer to her lap.

"The dates and times are registered in the metadata," he said, anticipating that as an argument from Crista, or possibly a defense later from Vern.

"He's hugging her." Crista zoomed the view out.

"And here he's kissing her." Jackson reached over to scroll to the next photo.

"It doesn't look brotherly," she said.

"It's not."

"This is hard to accept."

A female television announcer caught Jackson's attention.

"The Fountain Lake Family Hotel was the scene of a

structure fire this evening," she said. "Over three hundred guests were evacuated, while engines and firefighters were deployed from three stations in the area. Fire Chief Brandon Dorsey says that arson has not been ruled out."

The view switched to a reporter at the front of the hotel. He was interviewing a guest against a backdrop of fire engines and police cars.

"Is that code to say that it was arson?" asked Crista, her gaze on the TV screen.

"It means it's early in the investigation," Jackson answered honestly. But it was arson. He knew it was arson.

"Tell me the truth," she said, her gaze not wavering.

"He did it to get us both out of the building. He wants you back. But I'm guessing he also wants you far away from me."

She turned her head, looking surprised. "Why?"

"You have a mirror, right?"

She lifted her hand and self-consciously touched her damp hair. It was tousled and incredibly sexy.

"He thinks I'm your ex-boyfriend," Jackson reminded her.

"I forgot about that."

"He doesn't want the competition. I don't blame him."

If Crista were his, Jackson couldn't honestly say he wouldn't set a building on fire.

Looking unsettled, she turned her attention back to the laptop.

"I'm going to have to end it, aren't I?" Her tone was regretful.

Yes! "That's up to you."

She looked back at Jackson. "I don't think I can marry a man who's been unfaithful."

"I wouldn't."

"Wouldn't marry him, or wouldn't be unfaithful?"

"Neither." He felt himself ease closer to her. It was impossible to keep his true thoughts at bay. "Any man who cheats on you is out of his ever-lovin' mind."

She gave a ghost of a smile. "That's very nice of you to say."

"It's the truth."

Silence descended between them.

He wanted to kiss her now. He desperately wanted to kiss her luscious red lips. The robe's lapels revealed the barest hint of cleavage. Her skin was dewy from the hot shower. And he was all but lost in her jewel-green eyes.

"I guess I'll talk to him tomorrow," she said.

And say what? The question was so loud inside his head that for a moment he was afraid he'd shouted it.

"Unless there's some miraculous explanation," she continued, "I'm handing back his ring and walking out of his life."

"There'll be no miracle."

She nodded, twisting the diamond around her finger.

He gently but firmly took her hands. Then he slipped the ring off her finger, reaching up to place it on the table behind the sofa.

"But—" She looked like she wanted to retrieve it.

"Afraid it might get lost?" He lifted his brows.

"It's valuable."

"It's worthless. You're valuable."

His face was inches from hers. A small lift of his hand, and it was on her hip. Then he slipped it to the base of her spine. He leaned in.

"Jackson." His name was a warning.

"It's a kiss," he said. "It's only a kiss. We've done it before."

He gave her a second to protest.

She didn't.

So he brought his lips to hers.

They were as sweet as he'd remembered, hot and tantalizing. Desire immediately registered in his brain. Passion lit his hormones, while every cell jumped to attention. His hand tightened at the small of her back, drawing her against him.

He stretched his legs out, stretched hers out, and delved into the depths of her mouth. She kissed him in return. Her slight body sank into the soft bed.

Her robe gaped loose, and he knew it would take nothing, nothing at all to untie the sash, spread it wide, feast his gaze on her gorgeous body. But he held back, kissing her neck.

"Jackson," she groaned.

He loved the sound of his name coming from her lips. Her tone breathless.

"We should stop," she said. There was a no-nonsense edge to her voice now and he told himself to pull away.

"I'm sorry," she whispered, sounding as if she was.

"My fault," he readily admitted.

"I keep kissing you back."

"I keep starting it."

"These are extraordinary circumstances."

He summoned the strength and put a few inches between them. His eyes focused on her. "You are so unbelievably beautiful."

That got him a smile, and he felt it resonate through his heart.

"How does he do it?" He had to ask. "How does a man have you and even look at another woman?"

Her smile grew a little wider. "I can ask him."

"You should ask him. Better yet, I'll ask him. No,

I'll tell him. I'll tell him he lost you, and I got you, and I'm sure going to keep you."

"While you're still pretending to be my ex-boy-friend?" she joked.

"What?" It took a second for her meaning to register. "Yeah. Right. That's what I meant."

She sobered. "And then this will all be over."

Jackson wasn't ready to say that.

"I should be sad," she said. "I mean, I am sad. But I should be sadder. I should be devastated. This mess is my life."

"You'll be fine," he said.

What he wanted to say was that they'd fix her life. He'd help her fix her life. He was sticking around until everything was settled, until he understood exactly what was going on with the diamond mine and anything else that might hurt her. He was staying until she was completely safe from Vern and all of the Gerhards.

They slept apart. And in the morning, Jackson drove her to the shopping mall parking lot three miles from the Gerhard mansion.

"I'd rather come with you," he said as he passed under the colorful flags that marked the main entrance.

"He's not going to try anything with Ellie there." Crista was nervous, but she wasn't afraid.

Vern would have no choice but to accept her decision. He wasn't going to be happy. But surely at some level he would understand. His relationship with Gracie Stolt might not be a full-blown affair, but they were obviously intimate. Vern needed to do as much thinking about his future as Crista did about her own.

"He lit a hotel on fire." There was a hard edge to Jackson's voice.

"They haven't proven that yet."

"I have all the proof I need. There they are." Jackson angled the SUV across a block of empty parking spots toward a silver sedan.

"Whose car?" she asked, knowing Ellie drove a blue hatchback.

"It's a company car. Mac wouldn't risk taking Ellie back to her apartment for her car."

"They've been together all night."

"It's possible," said Jackson. "I didn't ask."

"So, you didn't assign him to protect her." For the hundredth time, Crista tried to figure out Jackson's motivation for sticking around.

"I didn't need to."

She tried to read his expression.

He seemed to sense her stare and glanced over. "What?"

"Why are you still here?"

He didn't miss a beat. "You've heard of pro bono?"

"That's for lawyers."

"It's for private detectives, too."

She didn't buy it, but let the issue drop for now.

He pulled into the spot close to Mac and Ellie.

"You know you don't have to break it off in person," he said.

"I want to do it in person. I want to see his expression. And it's the only way it'll feel final to me."

"I can come with you."

"Ellie's coming with me. Vern likes Ellie."

Jackson clenched his jaw. After a moment's pause he passed a phone to Crista. "I'm speed dial one. Call me if anything looks suspicious."

"Suspicious how?" She couldn't help but think he was used to higher stakes and higher drama than this.

She was breaking off an engagement, not spying on a foreign government.

"You'll know it if it happens," he said.

She doubted that.

He picked up the phone, waiting for her to take it in her hand. "If I don't hear from you fifteen minutes after you're inside, we're coming in."

"How will you know when we're inside?" She conjured up a silly picture of him on a hillside in camo and green face paint with a set of high-powered binoculars.

"That phone has a very accurate GPS."

"You can't storm the mansion, Jackson. They'll arrest you."

"They can try," he said.

"You're nuts."

"I'm cautious."

She reached for the car door handle. "We're going to be fine."

He put a hand on her shoulder, stopping her from exiting. "*Anything* suspicious."

"Yes. Sure." She would try. "I assume Ellie is getting the same instructions?"

"Mac's cautious, too."

"Okay." Crista took a deep breath and swung open the door.

The butterflies in her stomach had ramped up, and she told herself not to let Jackson rattle her. Yes, Vern was going to be angry. And if Manfred or Delores were there, the conversation would definitely get even more uncomfortable. But it would be over in a matter of minutes, and this would all be behind her.

As she rose to her feet, she wiggled the diamond ring that was back on her finger, checking to make sure it was loose. When she was nervous, her hands tended to swell. The last thing she needed was to break things off and try to give back the ring only to have it get stuck on her finger.

Mac stepped out of the passenger seat of the silver sedan. He nodded a greeting to Crista and held the door open for her.

"Thanks," she said as she slid onto the seat.

Mac leaned down, looking in the open door, his gaze on Ellie. "Don't forget."

"I won't," said Ellie.

He gave another serious nod then pushed the door firmly shut.

"Don't forget what?" Crista couldn't help but ask.

Ellie gave a sheepish shrug. "I'm not sure. The list was pretty long."

Crista couldn't help but smile. "Do you have a secret agent phone, too?"

Ellie tapped the front pocket of her white shorts. "I'm packin'."

"They've got us hooked up to GPS."

"I heard."

"And Jackson said we have fifteen minutes before they storm the place."

Ellie shifted the car into Drive and glanced back to Jackson's car as she pulled through the parking spot. "Who *are* those guys?"

"I can't figure it out. I keep asking him why he's doing all this, and I keep getting vague answers."

"He's hot," Ellie said with a glance in her rearview mirror.

"Jackson?"

"Mac."

That got Crista's attention. "Really?"

"You didn't notice?"

"To be honest, I wasn't paying much attention to Mac."

"I was." Ellie headed for the traffic light at the parking lot exit. "But forget about me. Do you know what you're going to say?"

"I think so," said Crista. She'd gone over a dozen different versions in her mind. "Did Mac tell you about the pictures?"

"He showed them to me."

"He kept copies." Crista wasn't surprised.

"They weren't fakes," said Ellie.

"I know."

They completed a left turn. Traffic was light, so they'd be at the mansion in about five minutes.

"Vern is pond scum," said Ellie.

"I keep going back and forth between coming out guns a-blazing or calmly asking for an explanation."

"Could there be any reasonable explanation?"

"Not that I can think of."

"I say guns a-blazing."

"Either way, the result will be the same."

"But not as satisfying. He needs to know he hurt you."

"He knows that."

"I doubt he cares."

Crista hoped he cared. The Vern she'd fallen in love with would care.

"Hit him with both barrels," said Ellie. "If you don't, you'll be sorry later."

"I have to at least ask him what happened," Crista countered. As far-fetched as it seemed, Vern might have something to say in his own defense.

"We're here," Ellie stated unnecessarily as they

turned in to the long driveway. "Are you sure you're ready?"

"I just want to get it over with."

"Then let's do it." Ellie stepped on the accelerator and took them briskly up the drive.

She wheeled through the turnaround and brought the car to the curb. A security guard immediately came out through the front door, obviously intent on asking their business. But when he saw Crista, he stopped short.

She got out of the car, pausing while Ellie came around the front bumper.

"I'm here to see Vern," she stated, holding her head high.

"Of course, ma'am," said the guard, his expression inscrutable.

For the first time ever, Crista found herself wondering if the guard was armed. Were all of the security staff armed? It seemed likely they would be. She couldn't even imagine what would happen if Jackson and Mac showed up.

"We need to hurry," she said to Ellie, trotting up the stairs. The phone in her purse suddenly felt heavy.

She'd been in the mansion foyer hundreds of times, and she knew it well. It was octagonal with a polished marble floor and ornate pillars. A set of double doors led to a grand hallway and the curving staircase. The hallway was a popular place for guests at the Gerhards' cocktail parties to gather and view the family art collection.

It had never struck her as intimidating before, but rather opulent and grand. It was fit for industrialists, celebrities, even royalty.

She heard footsteps descending the staircase. But she

stayed put, not wanting to venture far from the exit. It was Jackson's fault she was feeling so skittish. All his talk of speed-dialing him or him and Mac storming the place had her pointlessly nervous.

Vern appeared in the doorway, coming to an abrupt halt when he spotted Ellie. He frowned, and his nostrils flared.

"I asked Ellie to come," said Crista.

"I would have come anyway," said Ellie.

"She can wait here," said Vern.

"I'm staying here, too," said Crista. "This won't take long."

His brows rose with obvious incredulity. "What do you mean, it won't take long? We have our entire future to discuss."

"I've seen the pictures, Vern."

"What pictures?"

"You and Gracie."

He paled a shade, and she knew all the accusations were true.

But then he regrouped and went on the attack. "Do you mean Gracie Stolt? I told you, she's a client."

"She's your mistress." Then Crista rethought the terminology. "I mean, she would have been your mistress. If we'd gotten married."

Vern moved closer, his tone hardening. "You don't know what you're talking about."

"I've seen—"

"I don't care what you think you've seen. It was obviously a misrepresentation of something. And what about you? Shacked up in a hotel with your ex-boyfriend."

"I wanted to be alone."

"Alone with *him*."

"He was *helping* me."

Ellie reached out to touch her arm. "Crista."

Vern stepped closer still. "You're going to deny you slept with him?"

Crista opened her mouth to say yes. But then she thought better of the impulse. She had no need to defend herself. "I'm here to give you back your ring."

Vern shook his head. "I won't accept it. We can work this out."

"You just accused me of infidelity."

"You accused me first."

Anger rose inside her, and she jabbed her index finger in his direction. "You *did it*." Then she pointed at her own chest. "I *didn't*."

She grasped her ring and pulled. But as she'd feared, her fingers had swollen, and it didn't want to come off. She pulled harder. "But I'm going to," she said defiantly as she tugged. "I'm going out there right now to sleep with Jackson."

The ring suddenly popped off. It slipped from her fingers and bounced across the floor.

They both watched it come to rest on a white tile.

"You're not going to do that," said Vern.

"You can't stop me."

He reached out to grasp her arm, holding her fast.

"Let me go!" She struggled against his grip, but he wouldn't let her go.

In her peripheral vision, she saw Ellie retrieve her phone.

"Don't," she cried out to Ellie.

Jackson and Mac would only make things worse. They could make things a whole lot worse.

"Do I need to call the police?" Ellie asked Vern in a cold voice.

Vern glared daggers at her but then released Crista's arm.

"We need to talk," he said to Crista, schooling his expression, clearing the anger from his face, entreaty coming into his eyes.

"Not today," said Crista. She just wanted to get out of here.

"Not ever," said Ellie.

"You don't understand," said Vern, his expression now projecting hurt and confusion.

He suddenly looked so familiar. Her heart remembered everything they'd had together, and it ached for the loss.

"I have to go," she said, mortified to hear a catch in her own voice. She needed to be stronger than that.

Then Ellie's arm was around her, urging her to the door, picking up the tempo until they were outside. She immediately saw Jackson's SUV pulling up the drive.

"Are fifteen minutes up?" asked Crista, her voice now shaky. It had seemed more like three.

"You're going to sleep with Jackson?" Ellie asked as they hustled down the steps.

"I was bluffing."

"He didn't tell you about the hot mike?"

"The what?"

Mac hopped out of the passenger seat and jumped in to drive the silver sedan.

"Jackson and Mac could hear every word we said. Me threatening to call the police was the secret signal."

"There was a secret signal?"

"Go," said Ellie, pushing her toward the open door of the SUV.

Afraid to look back, Crista hopped inside and slammed the door shut. Jackson peeled away.

* * *

Jackson was relieved to have her back. He was stupidly giddy with relief. When Ellie had uttered the distress phrase, his heart had lodged in his throat. A dozen dire scenarios flashed through his mind as they sped up the driveway.

"You're okay?" He felt the need to confirm as they made it to the road.

"Ticked off," she said, fastening her seat belt.

"He didn't hurt you?"

"He grabbed me, but he let me go. His ring's on the floor of the foyer."

"Good," said Jackson with clipped satisfaction.

She shifted in the seat, angling toward him. "You bugged Ellie's phone?"

"We thought it was safest."

"Why didn't you tell me?"

"It would have made you nervous."

"I was already nervous."

"Yes." That had been his point. "It was bad enough for you without knowing you had a bigger audience."

"That was underhanded."

"Maybe."

"It was a personal conversation."

"You mean the part where you announced your intention to sleep with me?"

"That was a bluff."

It was too tempting not to tease her. "I'm very disappointed to hear that."

She moaned in obvious embarrassment. "Mac heard me say it, didn't he?"

"He did."

"Call him. Tell him I was joking."

"He knows you were joking."

"No, he doesn't. He's going to think there's something going on between us."

Jackson glanced her way. "There's not?"

"No, there's not. Well, not that. Not..." She seemed to search for words. "I just broke up with my fiancé. I was minutes from getting married on Saturday." The pitch of her voice rose. "There can't be anything between us."

"Okay," said Jackson. "I'll play along."

"I'm not asking you to *play along*. I'm asking you to accept the reality of the situation."

"Consider it accepted."

She watched him with obvious suspicion. "Tell Mac."

"Are you serious?"

"Yes." She crossed her arms over her chest. "I was illegally recorded, and I want the record set straight."

Jackson struggled not to laugh. "Sure." He fished his phone out of his pocket, pressing the speed dial and putting it on hands-free. He dropped it on the seat between them.

"What's up?" came Mac's answer over the small speaker.

"Crista wants me to set the record straight."

"What record?" asked Mac.

"She's not going to sleep with me."

There was a silence. "Uh, okay." Mac paused. When he spoke again, Jackson detected a trace of laughter. "Why not?"

"Because I barely know him," said Crista.

"He's a great guy," said Mac. "And I hear he's a good lover."

"From who?" asked Crista without missing a beat.

Jackson caught her gaze and mouthed the word *really*?

"Was it Melanie?" she asked, obviously thinking she'd turned the tables on him.

"He told you about Melanie?"

Jackson scooped up the phone and switched it to his ear. "That's enough about me."

Mac chuckled.

"Chicken," said Crista.

"We're not taking her home," Jackson said to Mac.

"Her being me?" asked Crista.

"Where to?" asked Mac.

"The office, for a start."

"Your office?" asked Crista.

"You want to look at the other thing?" asked Mac.

"That's right," Jackson said to Mac. "My office," he said to Crista.

"I should go home," she said. "This is over, and I'm tired of running. I'm pretty sure he got the message."

"He tried to physically restrain you."

"That was for her, right?" asked Mac.

"So did you," Crista pointed out.

Jackson didn't have an argument for that. He could also understand why Crista would think it was perfectly safe for her to go home. As far as she was concerned, she'd just broken up with a cheating fiancé. She didn't know about the diamond mine, so she didn't realize Gerhard and his family might have millions, possibly tens of millions of reasons to drag her back.

"I'm driving," he pointed out.

The car was going wherever he steered it. She could like it or not.

She crossed her arms and gave a huff. "If I'm going to your office, then Ellie's coming, too."

It didn't seem necessary, but he had no particular objection.

"She's my chaperone," Crista continued. "I don't want there to be gossip about you and me."

"You're obsessing," he said.

"Tell them," said Crista.

"Crista wants Ellie to come with us."

Mac's voice went muffled. "You want to stick with us?" He paused. "She's in," he said to Jackson. "I've got a couple stops to make. But we'll meet you there."

It took thirty minutes to arrive at Rush Investigations. The offices were housed in a converted warehouse a few blocks off the river. It wasn't the swankiest address, but the brick building was solid, and it gave them the space they needed to store vehicles and equipment.

They drove into the fenced compound and then accessed the garage area with the automatic door opener, parking the SUV in one of a dozen marked spots along the back wall. There was a customer entrance on the main floor of the attached four-story office tower. It was nicely decorated with comfortable seating, coffee service and a receptionist. But Jackson rarely went through there.

"Wow," said Crista as she stepped out of the vehicle onto the concrete floor. She craned her neck to look up at the open twenty-foot ceiling, where steel beams crossed fluorescent lighting, and her voice echoed in the mostly empty space. "This is huge."

Work benches stretched along two of the walls, while the east end was given over to shelving and a small electronics shop. An orange corrugated-metal staircase led from the shelving area to the second floor of the office tower.

"There are times we need the room," he said. "But most of the vehicles are out right now. This way." He gestured to the staircase.

"Just how big is your company?" she asked as they walked.

"It's grown since I started it."

"Grown from what to what?"

"To somewhere around three hundred people."

"There's that much going on in Chicago that needs investigating?"

He couldn't help a grin. "They're not all investigators. But, yes, there's easily that much going on. We also have offices in Boston, New York and Philly."

She stopped walking and turned to look at him, eyes narrowing, her forehead furrowing. "I know I keep asking this, but what exactly are you doing?"

"A lot of missing-persons cases," he answered. "Security and protection. Infidelity's always a big one. And then there's the corporate—"

"I mean with me. What are you doing with me?"

He knew he had to tell her about the mine eventually. But he didn't want her to bolt. He knew she'd be gone like a shot if she had any inkling her father was involved.

"For the moment," he said, meeting her eyes and telling the truth, "I'm trying to give you some time and distance to consider your options."

"I did. And I just took an option. I broke it off."

"You have other options. Life options. Like what you do next?"

"Why do you care?"

"Because I've spent most of the last three days with you."

She was clearly growing exasperated with his talking in circles. "Which leads me right back to *why*. Who sent you? Why did you even come looking for me in the first place?"

"Somebody asked me a question about Vern. I got

curious. And then, I guess, I just kept wading deeper and deeper."

"I'm not your concern."

He found himself moving closer, lowering his voice, increasing the intimacy of the conversation. "I spend quite a lot of time wading around in things that don't concern me."

She shook her head at what she clearly thought was his foolishness. "You normally get paid to do that."

He gave a shrug. "There's getting paid, and there's getting paid."

"One more time, Jackson, I'm not going to sleep with you." She couldn't quite keep a poker face.

He took one of her hands in his and stepped closer still. "You sure?"

She didn't answer.

He brushed his lips gently against hers. "You sure?"

"Not really. I'm not sure of anything anymore."

"You can be sure of this."

He kissed her.

She instantly responded, and he wrapped her tight in his arms, slanting his lips and deepening the kiss.

She molded against him, her softness perfect against the planes of his body. Desire rushed through him, and he gave it free rein.

They'd stop in a moment. Of course they would stop. But for now nothing in the world mattered except the sweetness of Crista's lips, the scent of her hair, and the feel of her hand in his.

Something banged in the reaches of the warehouse.

He silently cursed. Then he ended the kiss, drawing away and smoothing the pad of his thumb over her cheek.

"We have got to get alone at some point," he said.

"I'm so confused." Her green eyes were clouded and slightly unfocused.

"I'm not."

"This isn't simple."

He understood that it wasn't simple for her. It was perfectly simple for him. He desired her, and she definitely seemed attracted to him. It was pretty straightforward and a very nice starting point.

"We don't have to figure it out right away," he said.

She gave her head a small shake. "I'm not about to start dating anyone."

He didn't see why not, but he didn't want to pressure her. "Okay."

"I'm going to work out my life."

"Where do you want to start?" He'd be happy to help.

"Cristal Creations. I need to start with the company."

"How so?" He knew she had three locations around Chicago. From what he understood, they were doing well.

"They're my jewelry designs, and I manage the stores. But I don't actually own them."

Jackson wasn't happy to hear that. "Gerhard owns them," he guessed.

"It's what made sense at the time. The family already owned the shopping malls where we opened."

"So he got his hooks into your business." Jackson shook his head with disgust.

"It was only fair," said Crista. "He paid for it all. I wouldn't even have a business without Vern. He backed my designs when no one else would. Did you see the episode of *Investors Unlimited*?"

"*Investors Unlimited*?"

"It's a TV show. The kind where you pitch an idea

and the rich people on the panel can offer to invest. I was on it a year ago."

"You pitched your jewelry designs to Vern?"

"Not to Vern. He wasn't on the show. Nobody there was interested. But after it aired, Vern watched it and contacted me."

"He made you an offer?"

"That's how we met."

The timing was right, and Jackson knew the information could be significant. The show might be a catalyst for the whole scam.

His needed to find out who knew what about Crista and when.

Seven

Crista and Ellie were alone in a big, comfortable room that Jackson had called the lounge. On the fourth floor of the Rush Investigations building, it had banks of windows on two sides, soft chairs and sofa groupings scattered around, along with a kitchen area stocked with snacks and drinks. Easy-listening music filled the background from speakers recessed in the ceiling. It was night and day from the utilitarian warehouse area.

After helping themselves to sodas, they'd settled into a quiet corner with a curved sofa and a low table. Crista had kicked off her sandals and raked her hair into a quick ponytail.

It felt like a long time since she'd been home, and she was struggling for normalcy. Bouncing from place to place with a man she barely knew, desiring him, kissing him, all the while wishing she could tear off his clothes, was not a long-term plan. She needed to get herself organized. She needed to get her life in order and back on track.

"I need to find a lawyer," she said to Ellie, zeroing in on a logical first step.

"At least you don't have to divorce Vern." Ellie fished a throw pillow from behind her back and tossed it to the end of the sofa, wriggling into the deep, soft cushions. "Is there something in your prenup about walking away? Wait, you didn't marry him. The prenup won't count."

"We didn't have a prenup."

The statement obviously took Ellie by surprise. "Seriously?"

Crista took a drink as she nodded. The cola cooled her throat, making her realize she was incredibly thirsty.

"But he's a superwealthy guy," said Ellie.

Crista was acutely aware of Vern's wealth. "I thought it was a show of faith. I was really quite honored."

"That's really quite weird."

"I know. Now, I have to wonder if he wanted to avoid the subject of infidelity."

"He knew your lawyer would advise a big settlement if he messed around on you. If he'd said no, you'd have been suspicious. But if he'd said yes, you'd have made a fortune."

"Assuming he ever got caught," said Crista.

"Maybe you should have married him without a prenup and then divorced him. You could have cleaned up."

"I'm not that devious." Crista wouldn't have even wanted that windfall.

"It would have served him right."

"The thing I'm worried about is Cristal Creations." Crista needed a lawyer to sort out the company. She wanted out from under Gerhard Incorporated as quickly as possible.

"It's yours," said Ellie. "He can't touch it since you never got married. But, hey, if he wants to split it, then he can split his business interests with you, too."

"The jewelry designs are all that I own," said Crista. "The stores are his. Well, his family's, anyway."

"The Gerhards own your stores?"

"They own the shopping malls the stores are inside. I need to get my designs out of there. I'd rather start from scratch than have to work with his family."

"You should definitely call a lawyer."

Crista gave a mock toast of agreement with her soft drink bottle. "Now that it's actually over, I realize how much of my life is wrapped up in Vern. How does that happen in only a year?"

Before Ellie could respond, Crista's mind galloped ahead. "I had six bridesmaids. Only one of them, you, was my friend. Five of them were from Vern's family."

"He does have a very big family."

"And I don't have any family at all. But five out of six? You'd think I'd have more friends."

"You do have more friends."

It was true. Crista did have other friends, some that she'd have loved to have as her bridesmaids. But Vern, and particularly his mother, Delores, had been insistent on including their family in the wedding party. Crista couldn't help but wonder if she'd made a mistake by giving in so easily.

"Good thing you had me," said Ellie.

"Good thing I still have you. All the people I socialize with now seem to be his friends, or his family—mostly his family."

Ellie frowned. "Count me out of that list."

"I know."

"I'm not his friend. I think he's a jerk."

"I wish you'd said something sooner."

"No, you don't."

Crista reconsidered her words. "You're right. I don't. I wouldn't have believed you."

"And I wasn't sure. I could have been wrong. He could have been a perfectly nice guy."

"Not so much." Crista took another drink. She was hungry, too. When was the last time she'd eaten?

She glanced at her watch.

"It's nearly three," said Ellie.

"I'm starving. Are you hungry?"

Ellie's glance went to the kitchen area. "We can probably grab a snack. This is quite the place."

"Isn't it?" Crista took another look around. The room was fresh, clean, with sleek styling and designer touches.

Ellie leaned closer and lowered her voice. "I get more and more curious about those two guys."

"Why are we whispering?"

"I think this place is probably bugged."

"Your secret agent phone?" It suddenly occurred to Crista that they might still be broadcasting.

"It's turned off now, but this is all very cloak-and-dagger."

"Very," Crista agreed, glancing around for surveillance cameras. "They seem frighteningly good at it."

"Do you think we can trust them?"

"Part of me wants to say no, but they've done nothing but help me so far."

"They came out of nowhere."

"True," said Crista. "But whatever this is, Jackson

isn't in it for himself. He's been a gentleman. He didn't take advantage, even when I—" Crista stopped herself.

Ellie sat up straight. "Even when you what?"

Crista wasn't sure why she was hesitating. She was an adult, and Vern was now completely out of the picture. "When I kissed him back."

Ellie's brow rose. "Back? So he kissed you first?"

"Yes." It was silly not to have told Ellie. Keeping it a secret made it seem like more than it was. And it was nothing. "Yes, he did."

"When? Where? How?"

"On the boat. And in the hotel. And, well, in the warehouse, too." Crista didn't think she needed to add that it was on the mouth.

"It was mutual?" Ellie seemed rather energized by the news.

"It was very mutual. He's a really sexy guy."

"Good to hear," Jackson drawled from the doorway.

Ellie looked his way, her eyes crinkling with amusement. Crista felt her face heat.

"Don't let that go to your head," she warned him.

"I'll try my best." His footsteps sounded on the floor.

She forcibly shook off her embarrassment and turned to face him. "You shouldn't eavesdrop."

His mocha eyes glowed with amusement. "Occupational hazard."

"That's no excuse."

"I wasn't making an excuse." He sauntered farther into the room, followed closely by Mac.

She refused to stay embarrassed. If Jackson didn't already know she was attracted to him, well, he hadn't been paying attention. And he'd probably long since bragged to Mac about what had happened between them. Crista was going to hold her head high.

"I've got to get home," she said, coming to her feet. "Or to work. I should probably go into work and start figuring out the future."

"You'd planned to be away for three weeks on your honeymoon," said Ellie, rising herself. "Surely you can take a few days off."

"You can't go home," said Jackson.

"Come to my place," said Ellie.

"That's the second place he'll look," said Mac.

"So what if he does?" Crista had no intention of hiding from Vern any longer.

"Take a vacation," said Jackson. "Get out of the city for a few days."

"That's not practical," said Crista. Never mind that she had her business to worry about. She didn't have any extra money to spend on a vacation.

"It's better if you're not here," he said.

"It's better if I figure out what happens with Cristal Creations."

"She needs a lawyer," said Ellie.

"We have lawyers," said Mac.

"Down the hall," Jackson added with a tilt of his head.

"There are lawyers down the hall?" Crista couldn't keep the amazement from her tone.

"Rush Investigations lawyers," said Jackson. "Good ones. I'll introduce you."

She hesitated. The solution seemed too simple. Could she trust Jackson's lawyers? On the other hand, she knew she couldn't trust Vern's lawyers. And she sure didn't have any of her own. It seemed likely that anyone who worked for Jackson would be squarely opposed to Vern.

And it would be fast. Fast seemed like it would be good in this situation.

"They won't mind?" she asked, tempted.

"Why would they mind?"

"Because they have real work to do."

"This is real work."

She made her way toward him, watching his expression closely, trying to gauge what he was thinking. "Are you up to something?"

"Yes."

His easy admission surprised her.

"I knew it," she lied.

"What I'm up to is providing you with legal advice."

"Funny." She leaned closer, keeping her expression serious. "Why are you doing it?"

"Because your ex-fiancé ticked me off."

"And that's what you do when you're angry? Provide strangers with legal advice?"

"No." His jaw tightened. An edge came into his voice. "That's not even close to what I do when I'm angry."

He was intimidating, and it unnerved her. But her attraction to him was also back in full force.

He seemed to realize he'd unsettled her. "I'm not angry at you."

"Maybe not right now."

"Not ever."

But she could picture it. She could easily picture it.

He gave the barest shake of his head. "Don't even think about it. It's never going to happen."

Two days later, Jackson held his temper in check.

He stared across the prison table at Trent Corday. "So

I sliced and diced and dissected everyone involved in *Investors Unlimited* looking for a connection to Gerhard."

He stopped speaking and waited, giving Trent a chance to react to the information he'd just tossed out. The more he'd uncovered, the more suspicious he'd become of Trent's involvement. He might not be certain how it had all unfolded, but he was certain Trent was somehow operating behind the scenes.

Trent returned his gaze evenly, his features perfectly neutral. "Why did you expect there to be a connection?"

Jackson mentally awarded the man points for composure. "Because the two events happened suspiciously close together."

"Vern Gerhard must have watched the show," said Trent.

"Seeing the show didn't tell Vern Gerhard about the mine."

"The show could have tweaked his interest in Crista."

"Interest alone wouldn't lead him to the mine."

"I don't see how it matters," said Trent.

"It matters," said Jackson.

For the barest of seconds, Trent's left eye twitched, and Jackson knew he'd found a crack. He could almost hear the wheels turning inside the man's head. Trent desperately wanted to know how much Jackson knew.

Jackson didn't know much. But he pretended he did, putting a smug expression on his face, hoping to draw out something more. "It wasn't somebody inside the show," he said, lacing his voice with confidence and conviction. "It was somebody who already knew about the mine."

"No telling who all knew about the mine."

"No telling," Jackson agreed. "But we both know one person who did."

"Who's that?"

"You." Jackson tossed a copy of a call list on the table in front of Trent.

Trent's gaze narrowed in wariness. "What's this?"

"It's a record of calls incoming to Manfred Gerhard's private line."

Trent didn't respond.

"It's from three days before *Investors Unlimited* aired the episode with Crista."

Jackson hoped Trent would react, but he didn't.

Instead, Trent calmly turned the list to face him. He stared at it for a long moment. Then he sat back and crossed his arms over his chest. "You seem to be making some kind of point."

Jackson indicated a line on the statement. "My point is that call, right there. It's from a prison pay phone, *this* prison's pay phone. You called Gerhard before the show."

Trent pretended to be affronted. "I most certainly did not."

"They record those calls," Jackson reminded him. "I can easily pull the recording."

"The call was made at ten forty-five on a Tuesday," said Trent. "I work in the laundry until noon. I couldn't have made the call."

"This was a year ago."

"I've been working in the laundry for two years. Ask anyone."

Jackson studied the confidence in Trent's expression. He reluctantly concluded Trent hadn't made the call. But he was definitely hiding something.

Jackson leaned forward. "What aren't you telling me?"

"Nothing."

The exchange was getting him nowhere. What Jackson needed was leverage, but he didn't have any.

"You want me to protect Crista?" He played his only card.

He gambled that Trent cared at least a little bit about his daughter. If he didn't, he wouldn't have contacted Jackson in the first place.

"Crista's fine," said Trent. "The wedding's been called off."

"The wedding might be off," said Jackson. "But Gerhard's not dead. He still wants what he wants."

"You don't know anything about it."

"But you do?"

Trent's face twitched a second time.

Jackson pressed his advantage. "I can walk right now, or I can watch her awhile longer. You screw with me, I walk."

Trent stilled, obviously weighing his options.

"Stop trying to play me," said Jackson. "The truth is your only option."

"I didn't call the Gerhards," said Trent.

"Then tell me what you did. Tell me what I need to know, or I'm out of here and Crista's on her own."

To punctuate his threat, Jackson started to rise.

"Fine," Trent snapped. "It was me. I told a guy about the mine. But I had no choice. I had to."

Jackson felt his blood pressure rise, while his tone went cold. "There's always a choice." He couldn't believe Trent would endanger his own daughter.

"They threatened to kill me."

"Why?"

Trent started talking fast. "I owed some guys some money. The deal was to offer her a discount price and pocket the difference. That's all it was. I swear."

"What guys?" Jackson demanded. "Who did you owe?"

Trent hesitated.

Jackson started to stand again.

"It was the Gerhards, okay? It was a land deal a few years back. I guaranteed their city permits. It didn't work out. They lost big-time, and they've been dogging me ever since."

The revelation surprised Jackson. He'd pegged Trent as a small-time criminal. He'd never guessed Trent was involved in this level of corruption.

He wasn't sure he believed it now. "How could you guarantee their permits?"

"I know a guy," said Trent.

"You know a corrupt guy in the permitting office who can be bribed?"

"The Gerhards have men inside the prison. And they *were* going to kill me. It was my only bargaining chip. I didn't think anyone would get hurt, least of all Crista."

"You painted a target on her back."

"And then I came to you when it looked like it would go bad. I came to you for help."

"You lied to me."

"It got the job done," Trent said defensively.

"They didn't get their hands on the mine."

Trent's gaze narrowed, obviously not getting the point.

"What now?" Jackson elaborated. "How are you going to pay them back?"

"I sold them information. About the mine. We're square."

"So, they're not going to kill you?"

"That was the deal," Trent repeated with conviction. He didn't look like a man who feared for his life.

But Jackson knew this wasn't over. If he'd learned anything from his father, it was that criminals didn't give up while there was still a prize to play for.

"It doesn't matter if they kill you or not, they've still got their radar locked on her."

Trent took a beat. "I didn't mean for it to go like this."

"Well, it went like this."

Trent swallowed.

"You're a sorry excuse for a father."

Trent didn't argue the point. He barely seemed to have heard the insult. His cockiness vanished, replaced by apprehension. "You'll look after her?"

"I shouldn't have to." This time, Jackson did come to his feet.

"But you will?"

Trent's emotional reaction had to be fake. But Jackson didn't care enough to lie. "I will."

Trent closed his eyes for a long second. "Thank you," he muttered.

If Jackson didn't know better, he might have thought the man was grateful. But he did know better. Trent was a self-centered, pathetic loser who didn't deserve any daughter, never mind Crista.

He pivoted to walk away, letting his frustration and determination take him back down the long hallway.

The minute he cleared the prison building, he pulled out his cell phone and dialed his friend Tuck Tucker.

"Hey, Jackson," Tuck answered.

"Got a few minutes to meet?" Jackson asked as he strode toward his car.

"Now?"

"If you can. It's important."

"Sure. Where are you?"

"Riverway prison."

"That can't be good."

Jackson couldn't help but smile. "I'm outside the wall."

"Glad to hear it. The Copper Tavern?"

"Fifteen minutes?"

"Meet you there."

As he started his car, Jackson placed a call to Mac.

"Yo," Mac answered.

"You come across anything on the Gerhards bribing city officials?"

"Bribing them how?"

"Building permits."

Mac went quiet, obviously thinking through the question.

"Did you find something relevant?" Jackson asked as he turned from the parking lot onto the gravel-littered access road.

Poplar trees swayed beyond the ditches, and clouds shadowed the sun as the afternoon moved forward.

"It makes sense," said Mac. "A few committee decisions were overturned in their favor last year. That's not unheard of, but there were more than what might be expected. Let me look into it further."

"Check on Trent Corday while you're at it. He may have had a hand in something bad at the city. Turns out he was the one who tipped Gerhard off about the mine."

"Why would he do that?" Surprise was clear in Mac's tone.

"He was in debt to the Gerhards and trying to avoid death or bodily harm."

"By using his own daughter?"

"Yeah. Getting the mine into their hands was payback for the debt."

Concern came into Mac's tone. "But they didn't get the mine."

"I know. Trent seems to think they're square anyway."

"That doesn't sound right," said Mac.

"Tell me about it. Did you get Crista and Ellie dropped off?"

"Safe and sound at the Gold Leaf Resort. Ellie's making spa reservations. Crista's arguing, but I think Ellie's going to win."

"I hope Ellie can get her to relax, take her mind off all this."

"If anyone can do it, it's Ellie."

"Good call. I'm meeting Tuck on my way back."

"See you when you get here." Mac signed off.

Jackson followed the expressway to the outskirts of the city, then swung off to cross the bridge and pick up the quieter streets that led to the Copper Tavern. It was a laid-back, comfortable sports-themed bar, with dark wood tables, padded leather chairs and good-humored staff that seemed to stick with the place for years on end.

It was easy to grab a parking spot in the midafternoon. Jackson left the bright sunshine behind and quickly spotted Tuck at a corner table. Tuck gave him a nod of greeting and signaled to the waitress for a couple of beers.

"Wings and ribs are on their way," said Tuck as Jackson sat down.

"Works for me."

"You're buying," Tuck added.

"You bet."

The waitress, Tammy, arrived with two frosty mugs

of lager. She gave Jackson a brief, friendly greeting as she set the mugs down on printed cardboard coasters.

"What's going on?" Tuck asked Jackson as Tammy walked away.

"I need a favor." Jackson saw no point in beating about the bush.

"Sure."

"It's a big one."

"How big? Should I have ordered lobster?"

Jackson coughed out a laugh. "It's a whole lot bigger than lobster."

"Lay it on me."

"I need you to buy something for me."

Jackson slid a web address across the table. "Cristal Creations. They have three stores in Chicago. You buy the company now. I'll buy it from you in two years. I'll guarantee whatever return you want to name."

Tuck lifted the folded piece of paper. "Why?"

"I need my name to stay out of it."

"No kidding. I mean, why buy it at all?"

"I know the owner," said Jackson.

"You mean you're sleeping with the owner?"

"It's not about that."

"That wasn't an answer."

"No," said Jackson. "I'm not sleeping with her."

"Yet."

"The person I care about is the jewelry designer, not the company owner. Gerhard Incorporated owns the company. The woman's had a falling-out with them."

Tuck pocketed the paper. "Anything in particular I need to know about that situation?"

"She was set to marry Vern Gerhard. She backed out. He's not happy."

"But you are?"

Jackson didn't bother to hide his smile. "I'm satisfied with the outcome."

"And now you need her to sever all ties."

"I don't trust them. They're dirty, and they've got to be after revenge."

Tuck gave a nod. "We've got a Bahamian holding company that's not doing much of anything right now."

"Can it be traced back to you?"

"It can. But it would take quite a bit of time and a whole lot of lawyers. I don't know why anyone would bother, especially if the price was right."

Jackson tended to agree. It was common knowledge that the wedding had been canceled. And Crista had been on network television last year pitching Cristal Creations. An offer to buy the company from Gerhard should look opportunistic more than anything.

"I really appreciate this," said Jackson.

"Not a problem. My brother's got Tucker Transportation humming like a top. I have to keep myself entertained somehow. So, why'd she do it?"

Jackson didn't understand the question.

"Why'd she leave him?" asked Tuck.

"He was cheating on her."

Tuck's tone went hard. "Nice."

Jackson knew Tuck's brother, Dixon, had been a recent victim of infidelity.

"Anything else I can do to help her out?" Tuck asked.

"Not for the moment."

"You think of anything, you let me know. Dixon will help out, too."

"Thanks for that."

"I'm serious."

"I know."

There was a moment of silence.

"The guy cheated on her *before* the wedding?" Tuck asked.

Jackson pulled out the photo of Crista. He handed it across the table to Tuck. "That's the bride. And, yeah, it was before the wedding."

Tuck whistled low. "Are you kidding me?"

"She's bright, funny…good-hearted. Gerhard's an idiot." For that, Jackson was grateful.

"Or blind."

"His loss."

"Your gain."

"Not yet," said Jackson.

"You want some pointers?"

Jackson turned his attention to his beer. "No, I don't want some pointers."

Tammy arrived with the ribs and wings platter.

"Can I get you anything else?" she asked.

Tuck spoke up. "Jackson needs advice for the lovelorn."

Jackson rolled his eyes at the absurdity of the statement.

Tammy took a single step back and made a show of looking him up and down. She put a good-natured twinkle in her eyes. "Show up."

"Just doubled your tip," said Tuck.

Tammy laughed as she backed away. "Enjoy. Let me know if you need another round."

"I don't need any romantic advice from you," Jackson said to Tuck as he reached for a wing.

"What's your next move?"

"She's less than a week from leaving a man at the altar. I'm not going to crowd her."

Tuck looked skeptical. "You've got to be honest.

You've got to be up front. Otherwise women can sometimes conjure up all kinds of wrong ideas."

"Just because you lucked out with Amber, that doesn't make you an expert."

There was a smug smile on Tuck's face at the mention of his new fiancée. "That wasn't luck, my friend. That was skill, sophistication and—"

"Honesty?" Jackson got the point of the lecture. But the situation with Crista had more than its fair share of complications.

"I was going to say groveling. But let's stick with honesty for a minute. Trust is the hardest part to win and the easiest to lose."

"There are things I can't tell her."

"Like what?"

"Like the fact that her father sold her out to a criminal enterprise over a diamond mine."

Tuck raised his brow in obvious confusion. "You're going to have to throw a few more details into that story."

"Years ago, her father put some diamond mine shares in her name. She doesn't know she owns them, but her father told the Gerhards about them to settle a debt. Vern Gerhard is after the diamonds."

"The Gerhards need money?"

"More like they want money. If they based their behavior on needs, they'd have stopped building their empire a long time ago."

"How many shares does she own?" asked Tuck.

"Four."

"Four," Tuck repeated, obviously looking for confirmation that he'd heard right.

"Yes."

Tuck raised his palms in incredulity. "What can they do with four shares?"

"It's a privately held company. There are only ten shares in the world."

"She owns 40 percent of a diamond mine?"

"Yes."

"Are there diamonds in it?"

"I'm told there are."

"You have to tell her."

Jackson closed his eyes for a long second. "I know."

He'd spent the past few days telling himself there was a way around it. But there wasn't. Jackson wanted Crista, and he wanted her safe. Gerhard might have walked away from a runaway bride. But he wouldn't walk away from millions of dollars in diamonds and an outstanding debt.

Eight

When Jackson's lawyer Reginald Cooper had advised it would take several days to assess Cristal Creations and come up with a plan of action, Mac had suggested a spa getaway. Crista had vetoed the idea of leaving town again. She was tired of running from her problems.

But Ellie had begged her to reconsider. She reminded Crista that they'd been talking about a girls' getaway and how it would give her time to think. Then Jackson had added that the owner of the Gold Leaf Resort was a client of Rush Investigations, making the weekend practically free.

With all three ganging up on her, Crista had finally relented.

Now, lounging with Ellie in the outdoor mineral pool, she couldn't say she was sorry. The breeze was strengthening and clouds were closing up in the sky, but the rock pool was deliciously warm. Lounging on a seat, sculpted into the smooth boulders, with a tall glass of iced tea beside her, Crista closed her eyes and emptied her mind.

She felt more peaceful here than she had in days, and her brain had slowed down enough for her to picture her future. Maybe she'd find herself a new job. She probably would have to find a job, at least in the short term. Crista Creations was about to be dismantled. Without the Gerhards' backing, the company couldn't afford retail space. But without Crista, there'd be no more creations to sell.

She knew her designs were the unique element of the company. Without her, Cristal Creations was just another jewelry retailer. And it was a very competitive market.

She'd keep designing. But she'd pull back, retrench, rent booth space at a few jewelry fairs, work on her website and try to build up brand recognition. She'd make new pieces in the evenings, setting up in her kitchen like she'd done for so many months before Vern came along.

She pictured the work space on the island counter, the dining table covered with supplies, her closets overflowing.

Her eyes popped open. "Oh, no."

"Huh?" Ellie seemed to give herself a shake.

"I can't believe I forgot," said Crista.

"Forgot what?"

"I canceled the lease on my suite. The movers are putting the furniture into storage next week."

"You're homeless?" asked Ellie.

"It's almost impossible to find affordable rent."

"You can stay with me," said Ellie. "The new sofa folds out. It's really quite comfortable."

"That's nice of you. But it's not going to be that simple. I need to work from home again."

"Why not wait and see—" Ellie's eyes widened, focusing on a spot behind her.

"See what?" asked Crista, realizing she'd suddenly lost Ellie's attention. She twisted her neck to look behind.

A cloud partially blocked the sun, and she had to blink to adjust to the light.

Then she saw him. It was Vern. He was pacing along the pathway toward them, and there was a smile on his face.

"How did he find me?" She wasn't exactly afraid, but she was annoyed.

Ellie rose in a whoosh of water.

Crista pushed to her feet, striving for a greater sense of control. She crossed her arms and pinned him with a level stare. "What are you doing here, Vern?"

"I need to talk to you." His tone was smooth, his expression open and friendly.

He was wearing a business suit, but he bent down on one knee on the cobblestones at the edge of the pool. "I hate the way we left things, Crista."

She'd hated it, too, but it was entirely his fault, and there was no going back.

She held her ground. "Go home, Vern."

"Not until you hear me out."

She firmly shook her head. There was nothing he could say to undo infidelity.

"I know you're upset," he said.

"Upset? You think I'm *upset*?" *Try angry. Try incensed.* Everything about their relationship had been a lie.

"I can explain," he said.

"Explain a girlfriend?" Now that she was rolling, she couldn't seem to stop herself. "You can explain having both a girlfriend and a fiancée at the same time? How exactly are you going to do that?"

Ellie touched her arm. "Crista, don't."

Crista struggled to calm down. She knew Ellie was right. She shouldn't be challenging him. She shouldn't be engaging with him at all.

"She's not my girlfriend," he stated emphatically. "It was just a thing. One of those short-term, stupid things. I panicked. I knew I wanted to be with you for the rest of my life, but I panicked. I thought, well, I thought as long as it happened before the wedding—"

"Stop!" Crista all but shouted. "Quit rationalizing. You cheated. And I doubt you regretted it at all. I think you were going to keep doing it."

"That's not true."

"It's entirely true." She was certain of it.

"I love you, Crista. I want to share my life with you."

"You don't love me. You can't love someone and not want what's best for them. You don't want what's best for me. You want what's best for you. And you're willing to sacrifice me to get it."

"That's the thing. I *do* want what's best for you. And I've learned my lesson. I told myself it wouldn't hurt you. If I thought for one minute it would have hurt you—"

"Shut up," Ellie interjected. "Just shut up, Vern. Leave her alone and go away."

Vern's tone cooled as he looked at Ellie. "This is none of your business."

A clipped male voice interrupted. "Maybe not. But this conversation is over."

Jackson had appeared from nowhere.

"How did you…" Crista found herself gaping at him in surprise.

"Well, well, well," said Vern, slowly rising and looking Jackson up and down.

"Goodbye, Gerhard," said Jackson. "Or do I have to call security?"

"So you're here with her," said Vern.

Jackson didn't answer.

"He's not here with me," said Crista. "He wasn't here at all. Not until just now."

Vern shifted his gaze to Crista, clearly trying to decide if she was lying.

She wasn't. Then again, she didn't really care what he thought.

"You don't owe him an explanation," said Jackson. He took a menacing step toward Vern.

"You want to do this?" Vern challenged, widening his stance.

"She wants you gone," said Jackson. "You can walk out or be carried out. It's all the same to me."

Ellie grasped Crista's arm. "Come on." She tugged, urging Crista toward the glass-encased underwater staircase.

Crista realized it was good advice. She had absolutely nothing left to say to Vern, and her presence was only going escalate the situation. She left the pool and walked briskly away, scooping up the towels and robes they'd left draped over a pair of deck chairs.

Jackson caught up to them at the elevator.

"He's gone," he said.

"I'm beginning not to trust that."

The elevator arrived, its doors sliding open for them.

"I don't blame you," said Jackson as they walked inside.

"I'm going to hide in my room now." At least there, people would have to knock.

"You and I need to talk." His expression was too serious for her peace of mind.

"Can it wait?" she asked.

"It's important."

"You can drop me at the smoothie bar," said Ellie, pressing the button for the third floor.

Crista braced her hands on the rail behind her. "You know, I was happy in the mineral pool. All my cares and worries were flowing away."

"Five minutes," he said. "Ten, tops."

"I don't want any more bad news."

Before he could respond, the elevator stopped on three, and the doors slid open.

"Mac's around here somewhere," he said to Ellie.

Ellie's expression brightened. "He is?"

Jackson grinned at her telltale reaction.

"Catch you in a while," said Ellie, and she stepped briskly away.

"She likes Mac," said Crista, happy for her friend despite everything.

"Mac likes her back," said Jackson. "He'll track her down in no time."

"Because he's a skilled investigator," Crista guessed.

"Because she's still got the GPS phone."

"You guys make me paranoid."

"It's healthy to be paranoid."

Their eyes met as the elevator rose toward the presidential suite on the twentieth floor. His gaze was soft, and a rush of awareness heated her skin. She could fight it all she wanted, but he seemed more attractive every time she saw him.

Exiting the elevator, the suite was at the far end of

the hallway. A set of double oak doors led to a spacious set of rooms with a dramatic bay window overlooking the spa.

She extracted the key card from her bag and swiped it through the reader. Jackson reached for the handle and held the door open wide.

"Do you want to change?" he asked as they entered.

She dropped her bag on an armchair and tightened the sash on her robe. "You wanted to talk?"

"I did. I do." He seemed to give himself a mental shake. "I really missed you."

She'd missed him too. And her feelings for him were getting more confused by the moment.

He was an extraordinary man. He was sexy and self-assured in a rugged and dangerous way. But he was also classically handsome. In fact, he could probably be a model. She had a sudden vision of him in a pair of faded jeans, shirtless on a windswept beach. She wanted to tear off his shirt so that reality could mesh with her fantasy.

"Don't look at me like that," his voice rumbled.

"I'm not."

He eased forward. "You are such a liar."

It was true. She was lying to him, and she was lying to herself. She was looking at him exactly like that. She was completely attracted to him and completely turned on, and she couldn't figure out why she was fighting it.

"I'm sorry," she offered.

"For what?"

"For lying."

He seemed to take a breath. Then he squeezed her hands, causing her hormones to surge to life, and she swayed toward him.

He let go of her hands. Then he reached slowly up

to cradle her cheek. He canted his head, easing his lips toward her.

"Do you want this?" he asked.

She was tired of lying. "Yes."

"Are you sure?" he persisted. "Because if we shut it down again, it might kill me."

It might kill her, too.

In answer, she reached for the buttons on his shirt, flicking open one, then another and another.

"I'm sure," she whispered and stretched up to meet his lips.

His reaction was immediate. He wrapped his arms around her, kissing her deeply. She molded against him, feeling the strength of his body and the thud of his heart.

He tugged at her sash, releasing the robe.

"I'm soaking wet," she warned. Her bathing suit was going to soak through his clothes.

"I don't care." He stripped the robe from her shoulders and let it fall to the floor.

Then he lifted her into his arms, her flip-flops falling beside her robe. "Which way?" he asked.

She pointed to the bedroom door.

He carried her through then closed the door firmly behind them, setting her bare feet on the thick carpet. The balcony door was partway open, a breeze billowing the sheers. Muted sounds from the pool area below rose into the room. The fan whirred, and dappled sunlight danced on the buttercream walls.

He brushed back her damp hair, raking his fingers through the strands. She tugged free the hem of his shirt. Then she finished with the buttons, removing his shirt to reveal a close-up view of his broad shoulders and tanned muscular chest.

"I was right," she muttered under her breath, then she kissed his smooth pec.

"Right about what?"

She was surprised he'd heard. "About you." She kissed him again, making a damp spot with her tongue.

He gasped in a breath. "In a good way, I hope."

"In a good way," she confirmed.

He slipped off the strap of her bathing suit, kissing the tip of her shoulder. "I was right about you, too." The vibrations of his deep voice penetrated her skin.

It was becoming a struggle for her to talk. "In a good way?"

"In a very good way."

He released the hook of her bathing suit top. It fell, and her cool, damp breasts tumbled free.

He stepped back to look, and his eyes turned the color of dark chocolate. Her nipples beaded and a bolt of arousal spiked through her.

"Gorgeous," he whispered with reverence.

"Not so bad yourself." She ran her fingers from his navel to his chest and across to his shoulders. He was satisfyingly solid over every inch.

His hand closed on her breast, and his smile faded. He caught her lips again and wrapped his free arm around her waist to draw her close, her bare chest coming up against his.

Their kisses seemed to last forever. She wanted them to last forever. The whole world could disappear for all she cared. She wanted this moment, these feelings, this bliss she'd found with Jackson to go on and on.

Her knees began to weaken, and she could feel her muscles relax. He kicked off his shoes and popped the button on his pants.

In a moment, they'd be naked. They'd be on the big

bed, and their inevitable lovemaking would finally come to pass.

"Protection?" she asked.

"I have it."

She took a step, the backs of her knees pressing against the mattress. She gave him a sensual smile and hooked her thumbs into her bathing suit bottoms. Feeling sexy and powerful, and loving the molten expression in his eyes, she slowly peeled away the bottoms, stepping from them, standing naked in front of him.

He didn't move. His gaze went from the top of her head to the tips of her toes and back again.

Her confidence faltered.

But then he met her eyes. "I'm in awe."

"In a good way?" she joked.

"You're stunning. I'm afraid to touch you. If you're another dream, I'm going to be bitterly disappointed."

Her confidence came back, and she smiled. "*Another* dream?"

"I've had several dozen." He moved closer, stepping out of his pants.

"That's good," she told him.

"It was terrible," he countered. "They weren't real, and they were wholly unsatisfying."

She wound her arms around his neck, coming up on her toes to kiss his mouth. "I'll try to do better."

"This is better," he said. "So much better." And then he claimed her mouth.

Their naked bodies pressed tight together. She could feel every ripple of his chest, every shift of his thighs. His palms moved down her back, over her rear, smoothing the backs of her thighs.

She moved her feet apart, arching against him, a throbbing insistence growing at her core.

"Oh, Crista," he moaned, burrowing his face in her neck, kissing the tender skin, his hands kneading her fluid muscles.

"I can't wait," she told him.

He produced a condom.

Seconds later he cupped her rear and lifted her up. She twined her legs around his waist, reveling in the friction between them. He kissed her, his tongue teasing her mouth. Her hands tightened around him, gripping hard as he pushed inside, completing them.

She moaned at the instantaneous raw sensations. This wasn't merely pleasant. It wasn't merely nice. It was brilliant and intense, breathtakingly wonderful. Ripples of ecstasy radiated through her. He'd barely begun, and she was flying away, flying off in a million directions. Colors exploded in her mind, and she cried out his name and catapulted over the edge.

He stilled, giving her time to breathe.

"I'm sorry," she managed, embarrassed at her hair trigger.

"For what this time?" he rumbled.

"I didn't mean… I don't know what happened. I'm not…" She wasn't usually like this.

He stopped her with a kiss. "That was amazing. I'm honored. And we can start all over now." There was a chuckle in his voice. "Maybe you'll do better next time."

She was about to tell him next time never happened. It never had. When she was done, she was done. But she'd be patient with him. He didn't need to—

His thumb brushed her nipple, and her body zinged back to life. Then he kissed her mouth, and the glow grew inside her.

Curious, she touched her tongue with his.

"Oh, my," she muttered.

He flexed his hips, moving against her.

Arousal teased her stomach, moving along her thighs.

She answered his thrusts, losing track of time all over again. Their lovemaking went on and on, and he took her to unimaginable heights, all but shattering her soul.

Afterward, they fell onto the bed together, him on top, her tangled around him. She couldn't move. She wasn't even sure she could breathe. She certainly couldn't talk, even though she wanted to tell him he was fantastic and she'd never had lovemaking like that.

Minutes slipped past while they both dragged in deep breaths.

He finally broke the silence.

"That," he said, "was all of my dreams combined."

Crista's chest went tight. Warmth radiated within her. She didn't know what happened next. She'd worry about that later. For now, all she wanted out of life was to bask in the glow of Jackson.

As Crista nestled against his shoulder, Jackson kept her held tight. All he could think about was how close he'd come to missing this moment. If he'd hesitated outside the church, if he'd let her walk through the door, if he hadn't grabbed her in that split second, she'd be married to Gerhard by now and forever out of his reach.

He'd settled a blanket around them, his instinct to cocoon them together. Faraway shouts from the pool below made their way through the window. He watched as the fan blades whirled slowly above them, dispersing the fresh outside air.

He wanted to order some champagne, maybe some strawberries. He wanted to lounge in her bed for hours, laughing with her, teasing her, asking about her childhood, her friends, her jewelry designs. But he knew he didn't have that luxury. He'd put this conversation off too long already.

She needed to know she was a multimillionaire and that Gerhard was after her money.

"The Borezone Mine," he whispered in her ear.

She tilted her head to glance at him, blinking her gorgeous eyes as her lips curved into a smile. "That wasn't what I expected you to say."

He brushed a lock of hair from her forehead. "You need to hear again that you were fantastic? Because you were fantastic."

She shook her head, her hair brushing his chest and shoulder. It felt good.

"But we have to have this conversation. Have you ever heard of the Borezone Mine?"

"No."

"I'm not surprised. A few years ago, some shares of the Borezone Mine were put into your name."

She didn't answer. Instead, she propped her head up on her elbow, looking curious. "Was it an accident?"

"I doubt it. But that doesn't really matter. The point is you own them."

"How do you know that?" she asked.

"Mac discovered it." Jackson hoped he wouldn't have to mention her father.

"Okay." Her tone was searching. "Should I give them back?"

"No."

"I don't understand your point."

Jackson pulled himself into a sitting position. "Thing is, Gerhard knows about your shares."

Her forehead wrinkled. "How does he know about them?"

"I'm not sure," Jackson answered honestly.

She sat up, tucking the blanket around her. "I think I know what must have happened."

"You do?" Jackson braced himself.

"It had to be my father."

Jackson was surprised at how quickly she'd worked it out.

But instead of angry, her tone turned worried. "Is it an illegal mine?"

"No. It's nothing illegal. The mine is in northern Canada. It's perfectly legitimate."

"If my father is involved in something, it'll be a scam."

"We need to talk about Gerhard."

She was clearly becoming impatient. "Do we have to? Really?" She spread her arms. "Right now?"

"He knows about the mine, Crista."

"So what?"

"So, he wants to get his hands on your shares. That's what this is all about."

She blinked for a moment, clearly parsing through the information. "Are you suggesting Vern was marrying me for a mine?"

"I—"

"Are you saying he felt nothing for me?" She suddenly sounded angry. She bounced from the bed, draping the blanket around herself. "Why would you say that?"

"I want you to be safe."

"It was something, Jackson. I'm not that naive. He wasn't faking our entire relationship."

Jackson realized he'd made a colossal error. He couldn't have picked a worse time to have this conversation.

"Let me start over," he said. "Or better still, forget it for now. We can talk about this later. I am starving."

"Oh, no." She vehemently shook her head. "I want you to finish telling me how my fiancé suckered me and strung me along for a year to get his hands on a few shares in some mine."

"I want you to be safe," said Jackson. "This is all about you staying safe."

"Since the wedding's off—thanks to you, by the way—I don't see how I'm not safe."

"Gerhard is not a nice man."

She lifted her chin but didn't answer.

"And neither is his father. The entire family is shady. We think they tried to bribe city councillors for building permits. Mac is checking into it now. And as long as you have shares in the Borezone diamond mine, you could be a target."

"It's a diamond mine?"

"Yes."

"It has to be a mistake."

"It's not a mistake," said Jackson. "It's easily verifiable."

Her anger seemed to switch back to confusion. "But the Gerhards don't need money. The last thing in the world that family needs is more money."

"I can't say I disagree with that."

"So why would they care about anything I have?"

"They do."

"That's your theory."

"You're right," he said. "It is a theory. But I know I'm right. They won't go away. They'll try every trick in the book to reacquire you."

"*Reacquire* me?" Her tone was incredulous.

"You have to trust me."

She sat down on the edge of the bed. "Why did you make love to me?"

The question took him by surprise. He wasn't sure what she was driving at, so he didn't know how to answer.

He went with the truth. "Because I couldn't stop myself."

She frowned. "You tried to stop yourself?"

"Not today I didn't." He reached for her hand, but she tugged it away.

"Are you after the diamond mine, Jackson? Is that why you've stuck around all this time?"

"I am not after your mine." He hated that she had to ask. "The mine has nothing to do with you and me."

"Apparently it has everything to do with you and me."

"I'm here to keep you safe, full stop."

"You don't even know me."

"That's not true. I didn't know you. That day at the church, I didn't know you. But now I know you. And I care about you. And I am not about to stand by and let the Gerhards get their hooks into you."

"They can have the stupid mine," she snapped. "I don't want it. I don't care."

"You should. It will help you get your business back."

"How? Why is this so important?"

"They're criminals, Crista. And they have absolutely no right to that mine or—"

"I don't care," she cried.

"Crista." His tone was hard, but he needed to get her attention.

"What?"

"That mine is worth a hundred million dollars. And you own 40 percent."

The color drained from her face. Her shoulders dropped. Then her arms wrapped protectively around her stomach.

Silence ticked by, but he was afraid to speak. He didn't know what to say, and he didn't want to make it any worse.

"That's not possible." Her voice was small.

He wrapped a gentle hand over her shoulder. "To Gerhard, you represent forty million dollars."

The words sank in. "He didn't want a prenup." She tipped her chin to look at Jackson. "I thought that meant he trusted me."

Jackson gave in to his urge and pulled her protectively into his arms. "That's what he wanted you to think. You're a kind, trusting person."

She smacked her hand ineffectively against Jackson's chest. "Why didn't you tell me?"

"I just did."

"Why didn't you tell me before?"

"You wouldn't even believe he was cheating on you. I needed you to trust me first."

"I don't trust you now."

"I know, but I couldn't wait any longer. When I saw him out there at the pool, I knew it was time for some hard truths."

"It's been two hours since you saw him at the pool."

"I know that, too." Jackson spoke huskily, tightening his embrace. "But I figured you were safe with me."

"Plus, you wanted to get me naked before you confessed."

"Should I apologize for that?"

"Are you sorry?"

"I'm not remotely sorry for making love with you."

"The mine has to be a scam," she said with conviction. "It's my father. He wants people to believe it has a lot of value, but it will turn out to be worthless."

Jackson knew differently, but he didn't want to fight about it. He could show her copies of the share certificates, but she might think they were faked. It was better to wait and have Reginald take her to an official government office.

"Even if it is a scam," he said. "Gerhard believes it's true. That's the problem."

"He can't steal something I don't have."

"He can hurt you while he tries."

"I'll stay away from him," she said.

"Good decision. Give me the benefit of the doubt, and I'll show you final proof when we get back to Chicago."

"All right. I'll believe it when I see it," she said.

"Fair enough."

Her brow furrowed. "I think that means your job will be done."

"My job will be done," he agreed.

"Will you leave?" She tipped her chin to look up at him, obviously struggling to be brave but seeming vulnerable.

"I'm not leaving."

He was very, very far from leaving. His job might be done, but that didn't mean he was ready to walk away. Not from Crista. Not by a long shot.

Nine

"All I need to do is to find a new normal," Crista said from where she stood on the edge of the green on the resort's par-three golf course. Her life might be in chaos, but with a little effort she could sort it out.

"I'm normal," said Ellie, lining up her long putt. "And you can stay with me as long as you like."

"Concentrate," Mac told Ellie.

They were on the fifth hole. Jackson and Crista were ahead by four strokes. Their lead was thanks to Jackson. Crista could putt fairly well, but her drives were terrible. Conversely, Ellie could send the ball arcing beautifully down the fairway, but her accuracy on the green was abysmal.

"I am concentrating," she said to Mac.

"You're giving Crista life advice."

"I'm multitasking." Ellie hit the ball, sending it wide past the hole to the far side of the green.

Mac groaned.

"Don't know my own strength," said Ellie. "Not sure why you'd be in a rush to find a new place to rent," she said to Crista.

"Why rent?" asked Jackson as he placed his ball. "The market's good right now. You should buy."

"Why is he allowed to give advice and putt?" asked Ellie.

"Because he knows what he's doing," said Mac.

"And he's not your partner," said Ellie with a saucy smirk.

"That's true," said Mac.

Jackson sank the putt.

"But mostly it's because he knows what he's doing," Mac finished.

"And I don't take orders from him," Jackson joked, removing his ball from the fifth hole.

"Neither do I," said Ellie.

"That much is clear," said Mac.

Crista moved to her ball marker, replacing it with her ball. "I'd take orders," she said. "If they were good ones. It's not like I've made great decisions on my own lately."

"Buy a house," said Jackson. "A fixer-upper with good long-term property value. It won't cost much now, and you'll make a nice profit in a few years."

"I don't have a down payment," said Crista, eyeing the line to the hole and the slope of the green.

"She gets to talk while she putts," Ellie stage-whispered to Mac.

"Because Jackson doesn't care if they win."

"You're way too competitive."

"Jackson's a wuss," said Mac.

Crista couldn't help but smile at the exchange. On

the golf course or anywhere else, Jackson was anything but a wuss.

She drew back and hit the ball. It bobbled through a hollow but then sank straight into the hole.

"Nice," said Mac.

Ellie elbowed him in the ribs.

He grabbed her, spun her to him and kissed her soundly on the lips. "Keep quiet while I putt."

Her cheeks were flushed, her eyes dazed. "Yes, sir."

"You're killing me." He kissed her again.

"You own a multimillion-dollar mine," Jackson said to Crista as Mac tromped onto the green. "A down payment is not going to be a problem."

"I'm not going anywhere near that mine," she said with a definitive shake of her head.

"You're being ridiculous."

"I'm being smart. Everything my father touches turns to garbage."

"It's legit," Mac called out.

"It might look legit," said Crista. "Trust me, the FBI will be at my door soon enough."

"Reginald can confirm its authenticity," said Jackson.

"Reginald is doing enough for me already. Besides, asking a bunch of questions will only alert the authorities that much sooner. I've got enough to worry about right now without getting involved in one of my father's schemes. I'm ignoring the stupid mine, and I want you to do the same." She stared hard at him, waiting for his confirmation.

His expression stayed perfectly neutral.

"Jackson," she pressed in a warning tone.

"Fine. No Reginald."

"He's in jail."

"Reginald?" asked Jackson.

"Very funny. My father is in jail for fraud and forgery."

"I know. We did our research. Nice shot, Mac."

Mac headed off the green, while Ellie returned.

"It doesn't give you pause," Crista asked Jackson, "that my father's a forger and a con artist?"

"My dad's done time, too," he said, his gaze on Ellie as she lined up.

"Seriously?" Crista had never known anyone else with a criminal parent.

"Embezzlement. He was arrested when I was thirteen. I don't visit him. I don't really like to talk about it."

"Does it bother you?"

"Not on a day-to-day basis."

"Do you worry you might be like him?" Crista worried about that for herself. She had half Trent's genetics. The other half was from her mother, who had married a con man. And now Crista had almost married a con man. That might be the most unnerving part of all.

"Do I seem like a criminal to you?" Jackson asked, an edge to his voice.

"I guess not. I mean, you're on the other side of crime. You fight it. Then again, that's still a bit of an obsession with the criminal world."

"Your confidence is inspiring."

"I'm only trying to be honest."

"I'm not a criminal, Crista. And neither are you. Our fathers made their own choices—bad choices, obviously. But we're not them."

"My mother married him," she pointed out.

"You didn't marry Gerhard."

Ellie missed the putt but got a little closer to the hole.

"I'm not buying a house," said Crista.

"I hate to see you spend your money on rent, especially since you'll be trying to build your business."

"I'll manage."

"Every penny you spend on rent is a penny you can't plow into Cristal Creations."

"It's still the most practical solution," she said.

"It might be a solution, but it's not practical."

"It's every bit as practical as buying a house."

"Real estate is a capital asset," said Jackson.

Ellie sank her putt. She let out a whoop and hoisted her putter in the air.

Crista grinned at her joy.

"See what happens when you concentrate," Mac called to Ellie, loping toward her.

Crista started for her clubs.

Jackson suddenly grasped her hand and pulled her back. "Hang on."

"What?"

"I have a better idea."

"I don't want to hear about it."

"It's a very good idea."

She turned, letting out a sigh of exasperation. "Can't we just golf?"

"Come live with me," he said.

She blinked at him in astonishment, certain she couldn't have heard him right.

"I've got three bedrooms." His expression turned reflective. "I mean, not that I'm suggesting you'd need your own bedroom. I like sleeping with you. In fact, I love sleeping with you. I'd seriously like to continue sleeping with you, Crista."

She replayed his offer in her head, looking for the punch line.

"It's a great plan," he said, his gaze darting around

her expression. "Gerhard would absolutely leave you alone if I was in the picture. And, really...you know..." His eyes lost focus. He had obviously gone deep into thought.

"Jackson?" she prompted.

When he didn't respond, she waved her hand in front of his face.

"I've got the solution," he said. "It's so simple."

"I'm not moving in with you."

They barely knew each other. Jackson had wandered ridiculously far afield in his ramblings.

"Marry me," he said, grasping both of her hands, his expression turning earnest.

She opened her mouth. Then she closed it again. "Uh, earth to Jackson?"

"It's perfect," he said in what looked like complete seriousness.

"Mac," she called out. "Something's gone terribly wrong with Jackson."

"What is it?" asked Mac, immediately starting toward them.

"Vegas," said Jackson, still looking straight into Crista's eyes. "We can take Tuck's jet to Vegas."

"Has he ever done this before?" she asked Mac.

Mac halted next to them. "Done what?"

"I'm proposing to her," said Jackson.

"Then, no," said Mac. "He's never done that before."

Ellie arrived in the circle. "What's going on?"

Mac answered, "Jackson asked Crista to marry him."

Ellie's face broke into a bright smile. "*Really?*"

Crista turned on her. "Be serious."

Ellie schooled her features, lowering her tone. "Really?"

"No, not really," Crista snapped. "He's joking. Or

he's gone round the bend. At the moment, my money's on round the bend."

"Are you all done?" asked Jackson, looking normal again.

"Is it over?" asked Crista. "Your fit of insanity or whatever that was?"

"It's a perfect plan," said Jackson. "If you're married to me, then Gerhard is forced to give up and go away."

Neither Ellie nor Mac disputed the logic.

"Perfect plan," Crista drawled sarcastically. "What could possibly go wrong? Oh, wait. I'd be *married* to a man I barely know."

"For a good cause," said Mac.

Crista turned on Mac. "You're actually going to encourage him?"

"You can divorce me if it doesn't work out," said Jackson.

"It's not going to work out," she said, an edge of hysteria coming into her voice. "Because it's never going to happen."

He continued as if she hadn't spoken. "Just like they do in a regular marriage."

It occurred to her that she was being had. She glanced from one man to the other. "Is this a joke? Are you messing with me? Do you guys do this kind of thing all the time?"

They looked at each other.

"No," said Jackson. "I don't make a habit of proposing to women. I'd sure never do it as a joke."

She tugged her hands from his. "Fine. Whatever." She paced away and called back over her shoulder, "I'm going to tee off on six. Anybody coming with me?"

"I'm coming," called Ellie.

In a moment, Ellie was walking beside her.

"What was that?" Ellie asked.

"We were talking about rent and real estate. Next thing I knew, he was off the deep end. I should buy a house. No, I should live with him. No, I should marry him."

Ellie giggled.

"This isn't funny," said Crista.

"It is a little bit funny."

"No…" said Crista. "Okay, sure, it's a little bit funny." And there was some in the idea of marrying Jackson to keep Vern out of her life. "In an ironic way," she allowed.

"He must like you."

"Sure, he likes me. And he likes sleeping with me. Who wouldn't—" Crista stopped herself. She had been about to say the sex between them had been mind-blowing, both last night and again this morning.

"It was that good?" asked Ellie, a thread of laughter in her voice.

"We wouldn't get tired of the sex anytime soon," Crista admitted.

"I wouldn't get tired of Mac, either."

Crista stopped. "You had sex with Mac?"

"Why do you think he was there for breakfast?"

"I thought he came by this morning looking for Jackson."

Crista and Jackson had fallen asleep last night before Ellie had come back to the suite.

"You're not the only hot one, you know."

"I didn't mean—"

But Ellie was laughing. "Mac's pretty great. And he thinks the world of Jackson."

"Jackson seems pretty great, too," Crista said honestly.

"But you're not going to marry him?"

"What sane woman would do that?"

"Will you live with him?"

"No."

"It could be platonic."

"It wouldn't be platonic." Of that, Crista was certain.

"I've only got a sofa for you."

"Your sofa will be fine." They came to the sixth tee box, and Crista stopped. "Your sofa will be perfect. I am putting this crazy week—no, this crazy *year*—behind me. As soon as Reginald works out the details, I'll get to work on rebuilding Cristal Creations, and then I'll find myself a new apartment."

She selected the three wood, pushed a tee into the grass and proceeded to hit the longest drive of her life.

"The marriage proposal was out of left field," Mac observed the next day. They were back in Chicago at Jackson's house. Crista had moved in with Ellie, her belongings going to a storage unit in the morning.

"It wasn't the worst idea in the world," Jackson countered.

"It kind of was."

Maybe. But had Jackson pulled it off, it would have solved a whole lot of problems. And, truth was, the more time he spent with Crista, the more time he wanted to spend with Crista.

"You barely know her," said Mac.

"I know her better than she knew Gerhard."

"I'm not sure I see your point."

"My point is, she agreed to marry him, and he was lying to her from day one."

"That logic borders on the bizarre," said Mac. "You do know you're getting a little too close on this one."

"You think?" Even now as Jackson glanced around his living room, all he could think was how Crista would look good in the leather armchair, or on the sofa, or at the dining room table.

It wasn't clear what happened next between them. He was leaning toward inviting her over for dinner, a simple date. He'd break out the candles and wine, maybe order some flowers, do by stealth what he couldn't do with candor and get her to spend a night, or two or three.

"It may be time to move on," said Mac.

"It's not time to move on."

"She knows the score. She's not going to give the guy the time of day."

Jackson would agree on that front. But he still didn't trust Gerhard. And his gut said they didn't yet have all the pieces.

"It you want to date her, date her," said Mac. "But stop pretending you still need to protect her."

Jackson's phone rang.

He answered. "Hey, Tuck."

"We got it done," said Tuck.

"Cristal Creations?"

"Yes. They drove a hard bargain. Vern Gerhard would have walked, but the old man took double the estimated market value."

"Good."

"I hope she's worth it."

"She is," said Jackson. "Does she know yet?"

"Our Bahamian guy is calling Reginald right now."

"Reginald won't know Tucker Transportation's behind the purchase?"

"He won't. Do you want him to know?"

"No. And Dixon's okay with this?"

"Absolutely. I told him you were in love."

The statement took Jackson by surprise. "I'm not in love."

Across the living room, Mac grinned.

"Sure," Tuck said smoothly. "Keep telling yourself that." He paused. "Until you can't keep telling yourself anymore."

"You're nuts," said Jackson, and he frowned his displeasure at Mac.

"I know the signs," said Tuck.

"I'm hanging up now."

Tuck laughed. "Picturing her in a white dress yet?"

"Picturing her in Vegas." As soon as the words left his mouth, Jackson regretted them. He knew they left the wrong impression. But he also knew that explaining further wouldn't help.

"That'll do it," said Tuck. "I'll bring a jet if you let me be the best man."

"Goodbye, Tuck." Then Jackson remembered the magnitude of the favor. "And thanks. Thanks a lot."

The laughter remained in Tuck's voice. "No problem. This is the most fun I've had in weeks."

Jackson disconnected the call. "Tucker Transportation just secretly bought Cristal Creations."

"You know, you could do it the old-fashioned way," said Mac.

"Do what?"

"Date her. Win her over. And when she loves you back, propose."

Jackson rolled his eyes. "Give me a break."

"The barriers are out of the way. You don't need to be her bodyguard anymore. You're just two ordinary adults."

Jackson didn't know why he took offense to Mac's words. "She's not ordinary."

"And you're not in love."

"Let's talk about you and Ellie."

"I just met Ellie."

"Uh-huh." Jackson exaggerated the skepticism in his tone.

"Me and Ellie, that's me being your wingman."

"That's you falling for a beautiful woman."

"You're forgetting I didn't propose to her," said Mac.

"She's not the one in jeopardy."

Mac's expression turned thoughtful. "See, I can't picture that."

"Picture what?"

"Ellie in jeopardy. She's tough, and she's smart, and she'd take out any guy who tried to mess with her."

"Worried?" asked Jackson, glad to have the topic turned away from himself and Crista.

"Nope."

"Because you're tougher than her?"

"Because I'm not trying to mess with her." Mac's words rang true.

His situation with Ellie was dead simple. While Jackson's situation with Crista was anything but. He knew how she felt about her father. If he told her he'd been working with Trent, she'd never trust him. But if he didn't, their relationship would be built on a lie.

It wasn't a choice. To move forward, he had to come clean and take his chances that she wouldn't walk away.

Crista set down the phone, her brain reeling with the news.

"What?" asked Ellie. She was in the small kitchen of her apartment, tearing spinach into a salad bowl.

"Reginald says somebody bought Cristal Creations."

"What do you mean, bought it? How could they buy it?"

"They bought the company. From Gerhard. Reginald says I still have copyright on the designs."

Ellie frowned. "Is this good?"

"I think so. Reginald says they want me to keep running the company. He seems really excited about the sale."

"Who are they?"

"A group of wealthy anonymous investors."

"Does that strike you as a little hinky?"

"Should it? I do trust Reginald. He says holding companies do this all the time. And it's got to be better than Gerhard Incorporated."

"I suppose." Ellie seemed skeptical, but she went back to tearing the spinach.

Crista told herself to be practical rather than emotional. She fought an urge to call Jackson. She knew the sale had nothing to do with him. He probably wasn't even interested. Still, she found that she wanted to share the news and get his opinion.

"It's not like I have a choice," she said to Ellie instead. "I can't afford to buy it myself."

"How much did they pay?"

"It was confidential."

Ellie shrugged and turned to open a cupboard. "If it's more than fifty bucks, you couldn't have afforded it."

"I'm not that bad off," Crista protested.

"Oh, crap," said Ellie.

"What?"

"I forgot to buy almonds. The salad is going to be boring without them."

"No problem," said Crista, coming to her feet. "I'll pop down to the market. I could use the fresh air."

She could also use a little time to think. Her life felt like a pinball, bouncing off paddles, bonging over points, into traps, some things good and some things bad, but all of them on the edge of control.

"Can you grab a few limes as well?" Ellie called.

"Sure." Crista retrieved her shoulder bag.

The evening was warm, so she tucked her feet into her sandals and swung the purse over her T-shirt and shorts. She looped her hair into a ponytail in case of a breeze. Then she called goodbye and locked the dead bolt behind her.

The sun was setting on the street outside, lights coming on in the apartments above the shops. Ellie lived above a florist, which was next to a funky ladies' boutique and a toy store. There was a bakery on the corner with a compact grocery store opposite.

Traffic was light now that rush hour had passed. Neighbors and shoppers cruised the street, while laughing groups of people from the after-work crowd—or maybe they were tourists—sat drinking at the open-air café on the other side. The buzz of traffic, the aromas of yeast and cinnamon, and the bustle of ordinary Chicagoans on a Thursday night made her feel normal. It felt good.

She stopped at the corner, waiting for the walk signal.

The light was yellow, and a minivan with smoked windows came to a stop at the intersection. A silver sedan came up behind it. The minivan's door slid open and a man hopped out. Crista moved to one side so he could get around the light pole.

Suddenly, she felt a shove from behind. The man stared her straight in the eyes. He moved out of the way, and she was instantly propelled forward.

"Hey!" she shouted, angry at being jostled.

But the next thing she knew, she was inside the van. The door slammed shut.

"Stop," she shrieked.

A hand clamped over her mouth, and an arm went around her like a steel band. The horn honked, and the van lurched away from the curb, cutting around the corner to a chorus of horns from outside on the street.

A hood was thrown over her head, and sheer terror rocked her.

"Keep quiet," a gravelly voice commanded in her ear. Then he pulled his hand from beneath the hood.

She had no intention of keeping quiet. "What do you think you're—"

A hand immediately came over her mouth, pressing the rough fabric against her teeth.

"Quiet," the voice repeated.

She felt the car slow to a stop, and she screamed at the top of her lungs, hoping someone outside would hear.

The hand stopped her again, and the man swore.

"She pierced my eardrum," he shouted.

"Crista, stop," came another voice.

She froze. She knew the voice. And now she was more frightened than ever.

"Vern?"

"Nobody's going to hurt you," he said.

"What are you doing?"

"We need to talk."

"You're *kidnapping* me."

"You should be used to it by now." His tone was cool.

She kicked the back of the driver's seat. It was out of sheer frustration because her legs were the only thing she could move.

"Hold her still," came a third voice.

"Let me go," she demanded. "This is illegal. You're all going to be arrested."

"Like you had Jackson Rush arrested?"

The question caught her off guard. "He had his reasons."

"And I have mine."

"You can't do this, Vern. Whatever you think you'll accomplish, it's not going to work. You have to let me go."

"Get rid of her cell phone," said Vern.

She felt a hand dip into her purse, rummaging around. "Hey," she protested.

"Got it," said the voice beside her.

"Toss it," said Vern, his tone cold.

Her sliver of hope faded.

Jackson could have tracked her phone. When she didn't come back to the apartment, Ellie would get worried and she'd call Jackson. At least Crista hoped she'd call Jackson. And Jackson would have known how to access the GPS.

She heard the window roll down and the traffic noise increase, felt a breeze buffet across her, and she knew her phone was in the gutter.

She was at Vern's mercy.

She wished she knew what that meant. But the truth was she didn't know anything about him. The Vern she'd planned to marry never would have kidnapped her. He'd never have cheated on her. He'd never have terrified her like this.

Her throat went dry, and a chill took over her body. She was in the clutches of a stranger, and she had no idea what he might do.

Ten

"She's not picking up," Jackson said to Mac, his frustration turning to worry.

"Maybe she doesn't want to talk to you."

"Why wouldn't she want to talk to me?"

Jackson didn't expect her to call him the minute she finished talking to Reginald. Then again, he didn't see why she wouldn't call to tell him Cristal Creations had been sold and she didn't have to worry about Gerhard owning her company. Did she not think he'd be interested?

"It's only been ten hours since you saw her," said Mac.

"That's not the point. She's had some pretty big news since then."

"Maybe Reginald hasn't called her yet."

"He'd call her right away."

Jackson was sure about that. But he couldn't very

well call Reginald to confirm it. As far as Reginald was concerned, the purchase was a completely random act of an arm's-length company. Jackson intended to keep him thinking just that.

"You're obsessing," said Mac.

Jackson tossed his phone onto the coffee table. Was he obsessing? He wanted to talk to her. Was that being obsessive?

"Call Ellie," he said.

"And say *what*?"

"I don't care. Anything. Find out if Crista is with her."

"I'm going to look like a stalker."

Jackson picked up his phone and redialed Crista. It went straight to voice mail.

"Maybe she's talking to someone," said Mac.

"For forty-five minutes?"

"Maybe it's turned off."

"Why would she turn it off?"

"In the shower, taking a nap, in bed with—" Mac cut himself off.

"She's not in bed with some other guy." Though the thought did make Jackson's stomach churn. "You have to call Ellie."

"Fine," Mac said in a clipped voice. He dialed with his thumb. "If I'm going to look stupid, just so you know, you'll owe me."

Jackson nodded.

"Hey, Ellie," Mac said into his phone.

Jackson couldn't help but notice Mac's voice changed when he talked to Ellie, going deeper, smoother, more intimate. He obviously liked Ellie more than he was letting on.

"Really?" Mac's tone turned to alert, causing Jackson to look up. "When?"

"What?" Jackson asked.

Mac's look was intent and focused. "Did you call her?"

Adrenaline rushed into Jackson's system, and he came to his feet.

Mac stood. "We'll come to you."

"What?" Jackson all but shouted.

"Sit tight," said Mac, signing off. "Crista went to the store and didn't come back."

"When?" Jackson asked, his feet already taking him to the door.

"Over an hour. Ellie said she was about to call us."

"What store?" asked Jackson. "Driving, walking?"

"Two blocks from Ellie's apartment. She walked."

Jackson swore as he flung open his front door.

"We don't know anything for sure," said Mac.

"He's got her," said Jackson.

"That's a pretty bold move."

"I shouldn't have left her alone."

"You can't watch her for the rest of her life."

"I could have watched her for the rest of the week." Jackson would have considered the rest of her life. He realized he'd have seriously considered sticking right by her side forever if it would keep her safe.

"You want me to drive?" asked Mac.

"No, I don't want you to drive." The last thing in the world Jackson could do right now was sit idle.

"Jackson, we have to treat this as just another case. Emotion is clouding your judgment."

"My judgment is fine." Jackson wrenched open the door of the SUV. "Call Ellie back," he told Mac as he peeled out of the driveway. "Get whatever details you can."

Jackson pressed on the accelerator, racking his brain. Where would they take her? It wouldn't be the mansion. That was too obvious. Maybe to one of their businesses, one of their construction sites. Would they threaten her? Would she defy them? He was terrified she would.

Then he had an idea. He dialed Rush Investigations, getting the night shift to ping her phone location. It took only moments to learn the phone was southeast of Ellie's.

Jackson disconnected. "Her phone is at Edwards and Ninety-Fifth. It's stationary."

"They ditched it," said Mac.

"Likely."

"They had to know you'd check."

Jackson smacked his hand down on the steering wheel. They could easily have changed directions right after they tossed her phone.

He took an abrupt right turn.

"Where to?" asked Mac.

"The office. Call ahead. I want a list of every known Gerhard vehicle. Give them Ellie's address. Get them to canvass local businesses for security footage. Cross-reference vehicles on Ellie's street at the time to the place where the phone was dumped."

"Roger that," said Mac, disconnecting from Ellie.

At least it was something. If they could find a vehicle that had been in both places, maybe they could get make and model or even a license plate. If they could, they had a chance of tracking it farther.

"And Gerhard's buildings," said Jackson, his brain clicking along as he drove. "Locate *all* of his buildings. I want it mapped out by the time we get there."

They were going to need intelligence, and they were
going to need reinforcements.

"Will do, boss," said Mac. Then he began relaying
instructions to the Rush Investigations office.

Jackson sped up.

When they removed the hood, Crista found she was
in a warehouse. It was cold and hard, with concrete
floors, metal walls and high, open ceilings. The few
fluorescent lights that buzzed suspended from the cross-
beams did little to dispel the shadows. The cavernous
room was full of rusting shelves and aging steel bins,
with stacks of old lumber piled helter-skelter along the
far wall.

They'd sat her in an old folding chair next to a bat-
tered wooden table and three other chairs. They'd tied
her hands behind her back. But at least she could see
now.

Vern stood in front her, along with his father, Manfred, and a craggy-faced man she didn't recognize. She
could see two guards at a nearby door, their backs to
her.

"What do you want?" she demanded of Vern.

Part of her was terrified, but another part found the
entire situation too absurd to be taken seriously. It was
as if Vern and Manfred were both playacting. And for
a hysterical moment, she thought she might laugh out
loud.

But then the moment passed, and she shivered from
the cold and fear. Nobody was playacting. She was in
genuine danger.

"I want you to marry me," said Vern in a matter-of-
fact voice.

The statement struck her as beyond ridiculous.

"Right here, right now," he continued, glancing at the craggy-faced man. "If you do that, I promise to give you a divorce in a couple of months."

Manfred cleared his throat.

"Six months, tops," said Vern.

"I'm not marrying you," she said. "You cheated on me. You lied to me. You just kidnapped me, and you have me tied up in a warehouse." Her voice rose to an almost hysterical pitch. "I don't know what passes for romance in this dysfunctional family, but I assure you this isn't doing it for me."

Manfred raised his arm as if he was going to backhand her.

She braced herself.

But Vern stepped forward and grabbed Manfred's hand. It was the first time she'd ever seen him stand up to his father. She found herself astonished.

"That's not necessary," said Vern.

"Make her listen," Manfred hissed.

"You need to marry me," said Vern, his tone going earnest.

She kept silent. Tears burned in the corners of her eyes.

"You have two choices," said Manfred, both his voice and his expression more intimidating than she'd ever seen. "Marry my boy now. Sail the Mediterranean just like you planned. Work on your tan, enjoy the food, drink the wine. He'll divorce you soon enough."

"And keep my diamond mine," she dared to say.

"And keep your mine," Manfred agreed, not seeming surprised that she knew.

"You know it's bogus," she said.

Both men looked confused.

"I don't know how you know about it, but my father's

a con artist. He will have set this up for some convoluted reason of his own. There is no mine. And if there is, it doesn't have any diamonds."

Manfred gave a chilling smile. "Oh, there's a mine, all right."

Crista shook her head. "This is pointless."

"If there's no mine," Vern added reasonably, "then there's nothing for you to protect."

"I'm not marrying you," she said.

Mine or no mine, she wouldn't promise to love and honor Vern. She'd dodged that bullet when Jackson grabbed her outside the church, and she wasn't about to throw herself back in front of it.

Jackson had shown her the truth about her fiancé. He'd shown her the truth about other things, too, like how amazing and trusting a relationship could be between two people. Despite how it had started, in such a short time, she felt closer to Jackson than she'd ever felt to Vern.

She could be herself with Jackson, her total candid self. He didn't mind if she was opinionated. He didn't mind if she argued. He even knew about her father, and he hadn't pitied her. He'd understood. He understood her embarrassment, her anger, even her denial in a way few other people could.

She suddenly missed him with all her heart. She realized she should have said yes to staying at his place. For a crazy moment, she even wished she'd married him. Maybe they'd be in Vegas right now having an outlandish honeymoon in a garish hotel, playing poker or watching a circus act.

"That brings us to choice number two," said Manfred, making a show of inspecting his manicure as he spoke.

Her thoughts of Jackson vanished, and her fear returned. The ropes were tight around her wrists, chafing her skin. And she was growing colder by the minute. It was clear that Manfred was perfectly willing to have her suffer.

"We sign the papers for you," he said, his expression remorseless.

"What papers?" She couldn't help but ask. She looked from Manfred to Vern.

"Hans over there is a very good forger."

"For the mine?" she asked. Did they want her to sign over ownership of the mine? She'd do it. She was positive there was nothing to lose in that.

Manfred clicked his teeth as he waggled a finger at her. "Oh, no, that would be too suspicious. Hans will sign the marriage license for you."

Crista drew back in the metal chair. Their plan was to forge a marriage license. Exactly how did they expect that to work? She'd only deny it the minute they let her go.

"Then it's off on your honeymoon," said Manfred, sounding like he was enjoying himself. "Only to perish in a very tragic drowning accident off the yacht."

She stilled. Had Manfred just threatened to kill her? Did he expect her to believe him?

She found herself looking to Vern again, searching for the man who'd held her so tenderly. They'd danced. They'd laughed. She'd commiserated with him over his unbending father. He'd proposed on one knee with candlelight and roses.

"You're not throwing me overboard," she said to him. There was no way she'd believe that.

"We don't have a prenup," said Vern, sounding frighteningly practical. "Our wills were drafted weeks ago. It would be tragic, but it would be completely believable."

A sick feeling welled up inside her. "I already told you, the mine's a fake. Take it. It's not about the mine. It's about not wanting to marry you."

"Give me a break," Vern scoffed.

"What about when—" Crista stopped herself. She'd been about to point out that Ellie would go to the authorities. She wouldn't for a second believe Crista had willingly married Vern.

But saying it out loud would only put Ellie in danger. The last thing she wanted to do was hurt Ellie.

As her fear grew to unbearable heights, suddenly a loud crash reverberated through the warehouse. Men shouted over the sound of running feet. Manfred turned, while Vern and the craggy man turned pale. Everything was in motion around her.

Vern grabbed her, pulling her to her feet.

"Let her go!" Jackson shouted.

Crista wanted to whoop and cheer. Mac was there. So were a bunch of other men. The Gerhards' security guards seemed stunned, too.

"Let her go," Jackson repeated and began pacing toward them.

"Don't come any closer," Vern growled, waving a gun.

"Jackson," she cried, both relieved and newly terrified.

"Walk away from this," Manfred commanded.

"Not going to happen," said Jackson.

Crista focused on Jackson, trying to send a message with her eyes. She was grateful he was here. She was so glad to see him. She didn't see a way out, but she hoped he had a plan.

She started to work on the knots, hoping to free her hands from the rope and be ready.

"He's here for the mine himself," said Vern. "Nothing more, nothing less."

"I'm here for Crista," said Jackson.

"You didn't think we'd find out?" asked Vern.

"I don't care what you think you know," Jackson spat.

"He wants the diamonds every bit as much as I want the diamonds," said Vern.

"There *are* no diamonds," Crista shouted. Why wouldn't anyone listen to her?

"Did you ever ask him how he knew?" asked Vern.

Jackson took a step forward.

Vern pulled her tighter, jabbing her with the gun.

"Ask who sent him. Ask him how he knows your daddy's cell mate. Ask him how many times he met with Trent Corday before he dragged you from our wedding."

Jackson's jaw hardened, and his nostrils flared. But he didn't deny the accusations.

Crista tried to make some sense out of it. "You know my father?"

"What was the deal?" Vern asked Jackson. "Were you going to split it fifty-fifty?"

"It's complicated," Jackson said to Crista.

Her heart sank. At the same time, her hands came free of the rope.

"What was the plan?" repeated Vern. "Were you going to marry her instead?"

Crista withered.

Jackson's frown deepened.

Vern laughed out loud. "Oh, that's too rich. You already asked her to marry you? You couldn't even wait, say, a month or so, to let the dust settle?"

"I was protecting her from you."

"You were conning her *yourself.*" Vern's tone went lower, speaking to Crista. "His father is your father's cell mate. Colin Rush, the king of the Ponzi scheme. His daddy makes your daddy look like a carnival huckster. He's here for the diamonds. He doesn't give a damn about you."

"Shut up," Jackson shouted, striding forward.

Crista wrenched herself from Vern's arms.

"Crista—" Jackson began.

"You stay away," she warned him. She glanced around the room. "Everybody *stay far away from me.*"

She refused to be taken in by anybody. She stopped in front of Mac. "Give me your car keys."

"You sure?"

"I'm sure. And your cash. Give me all of your cash." It was on the tip of her tongue to tell him she'd pay him back. But given the circumstances, it seemed silly to be polite.

Mac gave a small smile. "Smart girl."

"I've learned a few things along the way."

"Let me explain," Jackson pleaded with her.

She dared to look at him. "So you can tell me more lies?"

She was heartsick at his deception. Her father had sent him. She'd been such an easy mark. She'd been a laughably easy mark.

"It wasn't lies," said Jackson.

"Do you know my father?"

Jackson's nostrils flared. "Yes."

"He sent you?" She already knew the answer.

"Yes."

"He told you about the diamond mine."

"Yes, but—"

"Joke's on you, Jackson. Trent conned you just like

he's conned everybody his whole life. The mine doesn't exist."

"Mac confirmed it," said Jackson.

Crista barked out a laugh. "He thinks he confirmed it. That just says my father is one step ahead of Mac."

She turned her attention to Mac, who was reaching into his pockets. He handed her the keys and a wad of cash.

"What are you doing?" Jackson demanded of Mac.

"Letting her go," Mac said mildly.

"No," Jackson shouted.

Mac gave him a look.

"Right," said Jackson, clenching his jaw. "You're right. She needs to get out of here."

"Norway," he said to the man closest to him, "give her all your money."

The man called Norway didn't hesitate. He pulled a wad of cash out of his pocket and handed it over.

"Dump Mac's car at the bus station," said Jackson, coming close. "You lay low for a while until we clear this up."

"I know what I'm doing," said Crista. She was going to disappear into anonymity. And it was going to be for more than just a while. None of them would find her until she wanted to be found. "You'll keep Vern from coming after me?" she asked Jackson.

"Absolutely," he said.

"Good." Crista stuffed the money into the pocket of her shorts. "Tell Ellie not to worry."

Crista headed for the door.

She located Mac's SUV and started it up. She was doing exactly as Jackson had suggested. She'd ditch the vehicle at the bus station. But then she'd take a taxi to the train station, buy a ticket with cash, switch trains outside the city and find herself a quiet, budget hotel where she could pay cash and hide under a fake name.

She realized she couldn't trust Reginald anymore. But the Yellow Pages were full of lawyers. She'd find her own lawyer. Then she'd work her way through the changes at Cristal Creations all on her own. She was through depending on others for help.

Since calling the police would leave them all with a lot of explaining to do, Jackson assumed the Gerhards would keep the altercation to themselves. And though it chafed to let her go on her own, he'd made sure Crista had a three-hour head start on Vern.

Now, both groups cautiously crossed the parking lot, each watching their backs as the entered their respective vehicles.

Jackson wanted to search for Crista right away. He wanted the Rush Investigations team to head straight back to the office and get started. He knew Gerhard would do exactly that, and it killed him simply sit still and wait for her to come back.

"What if she's right about her father?" Jackson mused out loud as the sun broke the horizon, lighting the world outside the meeting room window.

"That the diamond mine is worthless?" asked Mac.

Jackson wished he could seriously consider that possibility, because no diamond mine meant Crista had no value to Gerhard, so Gerhard would disappear.

"No. Not that," said Jackson. "I'm convinced the diamond mine is legit. But that doesn't mean Trent's not running some other con."

Mac hesitated. "What con would he be running? What are we not seeing?"

Jackson scanned through the facts.

"Problem is you're not seeing anything beyond Crista," said Mac. "You get that you're in love with her, right?"

Jackson wasn't letting his emotions get in the way of solving this. He couldn't afford to do that. He ordered himself to slow down, detach, think harder.

And then it hit him. "Trent's lying."

Trent had initially downplayed his culpability in Crista's engagement. Not that Jackson was sorry about that part. In fact, he was glad Trent had lied to him back then.

"You think he's still lying?" asked Mac.

Jackson was certain of it. "The Gerhards aren't threatening to kill Trent. They're in league with him."

"That would be a cold-blooded move," said Mac. "Voluntarily setting up your own daughter."

Jackson whistled low. It was all coming clear. "Trent told them about the mine, and he told them how to get to Crista. Were they going to split the take?"

"Why wouldn't Trent just split it with Crista?"

"Crista won't even speak to him. She never would have trusted him."

"But why get cold feet at the last minute?" asked Mac. "Why would he call you in and mess it all up?"

"Because they double-crossed him." Jackson stood, absolutely certain he was right. "He didn't call me in to help Crista. He only wanted his leverage back."

Mac seemed to be considering what he'd said. "If that's the case, what's his next move?"

"I don't know." Jackson gripped the back of the chair, tightening his fingers, ordering himself to think carefully. "But she's his bargaining chip. He needs her back in his clutches."

"We better find her first," said Mac.

Jackson started for the door. "And Daddy dearest is going to help us do that. That creep is going to tell me everything he knows."

"He'll only lie," Mac called.

"Let him try."

It was a two-hour drive to Riverway State. Jackson made it in ninety minutes. For the third time, he found himself sitting across a prison visiting table from Trent Corday.

"What's your new plan?" he barked without preamble.

"My new plan for what?"

"For Crista. Don't bother lying. Nobody's threatening you. You're all the way in Gerhard's pocket."

Trent's fleetingly shocked expression told Jackson he was right.

"You sold out your own daughter," Jackson spat. "It was a setup from minute one."

"If they told you that, they're lying."

Jackson had no interest in debating the past. He was certain Trent had orchestrated the whole thing. "How do you plan to get her back?"

Trent's complexion darkened. "I don't know what you're talking about."

"You think I'm going to let him kidnap her again?"

"What? Kidnap who?"

Jackson was through with the man's games. "Playing dumb gets you nothing."

"I'm not—"

"What is the new plan?" Jackson articulated each word slowly and carefully.

"The new plan to *what*?"

Jackson wanted to take a swing. "Don't you know

that once they're married, Gerhard has no reason to keep her alive?"

"I thought the wedding was off." Trent looked confused.

Jackson wasn't buying it. "Your backup plan has a backup plan." He knew how these men worked. "If not a marriage to Gerhard for a kickback from the mine, then what? Who? What do I need to protect her from?"

Guilt flashed across Trent's face. "There was never any reason to hurt her."

"There was always a reason to hurt her. I know you're not burdened with a conscience, but don't lie to yourself. And stop lying to me. *What happens next?*"

"Nothing," Trent shouted. "I mean, I've thought about it. There are tens of millions of dollars at stake. And they're mine."

"They're Crista's."

Trent's tone went sullen. "She never even knew they existed."

"What's the new plan?"

It was clear Trent didn't want to answer.

Jackson waited.

"I haven't had time to come up with one," Trent finally admitted.

Now there was something Jackson could believe.

"Gerhard was my only play," said Trent. "I can't come at her directly. Crista has never trusted me."

"And thanks to you, she'll never trust me, either. Which only makes my job harder."

"What are you planning to do?"

"What you should have done in the first place."

"I don't understand."

"Protect Crista from the lowlifes you put in her path."

"How?"

"None of your business."

"How can it hurt to tell me?"

"You don't deserve to know."

Trent reached out to him. "I'm not as bad as you think. They were never supposed to hurt her."

"Are you saying they planned a divorce all along."

"Yes. There was no prenup to protect the mine, so all he had to do was divorce her."

Jackson couldn't believe Trent would be so stupid. "What about Gerhard's assets? Don't try to tell me he'd give her a settlement."

"It's all in Manfred's name. Vern owns nothing."

"Still, a divorce would mean giving her part of the mine. They wouldn't do that. You put her *life* at risk."

Trent paled a shade. "They said it would be a divorce."

"They lied, and you're a fool."

The two men stared at each other for a long moment.

"What's your plan?" Trent's voice broke. "Tell me how you're going to protect my little girl."

Jackson stepped back, releasing a long breath. "For one thing," he said, "Cristal Creations is out of Gerhard's hands."

"You did that?"

"I had someone do that for me. Tell them, don't tell them. It's too late for them to change anything. Tell them they'll never be able to get to her. She'll be protected 24/7 for a month or a year or forever, whatever it takes."

Jackson wished he didn't have to do all this in secret. He wanted to be honest with her. He wanted to be in her life. He wanted to *be* her life.

He was completely in love with her. It angered him that he was figuring that out in a prison. It angered him more that he was figuring it out while confronting her no-good father. The entire situation was thoroughly wrong and completely unfair.

"Why?" asked Trent, looking genuinely perplexed.

"Because she deserves it. She deserves everything."

Jackson rose from the seat. He was done here. He was done with Trent. He knew the truth now, but it didn't help him. He should have asked way more questions in the beginning. He should have been more suspicious. He might not have purposely conned Crista. But the result was the same. His stupidity had put her in harm's way.

Maybe he didn't deserve her any more than Trent did.

Eleven

It took Crista three days to figure out a solution. But she woke up one morning, and it was fully formed.

"Are you sure?" asked Ellie as they drove east from where they'd met up in Rockford.

Crista had set up an anonymous email account to communicate with Ellie. When she'd sent a message, Ellie had left Chicago, switching from a taxi to a train to a bus, while Crista had made her way from a boutique hotel over the border in Wisconsin.

"It's meaningless," said Crista. "And it's making me a target. Even if the mine is worth some money, I don't want it."

"But him? Are you sure you even want to talk to him?"

"He can't hurt me from behind bars."

"He hurt you by putting a diamond mine in your name."

"And I'm about to undo that. As soon as the mine is out of the picture, Vern walks away—and Jackson walks away." Crista couldn't help the little catch in her voice as she said Jackson's name.

He'd broken her heart. She hadn't realized how badly she'd fallen for him until that night in the warehouse. Anger had carried her for a few hours. But once the anger wore off, his betrayal had devastated her.

He'd seemed so clever, so funny, so compassionate and so incredibly handsome. She'd started to think of him as her soul mate. He'd comforted her. He made her think he genuinely cared about her.

She realized now that her upbringing had left her starved for male attention. It seemed she was willing to take a chance on anyone, including Vern and Jackson. It was entirely understandable, but it was also foolish. And she would never make that mistake again.

"I don't mean the money," said Ellie. "Cristal Creations is going to be wildly successful. I mean, seeing your father in person, talking to him, having him try to manipulate you into… I don't know. But whatever it is, it's going to upset you."

"I'm immune," said Crista.

She'd done nothing for the last three days but be angry with her father, detest Vern and build a wall against her feelings for Jackson. She dared any of the three of them to try to get under her skin.

"I hope so," said Ellie.

"It'll take five minutes," said Crista. "All I need is his signature on the legal papers, and the mine is all his. He can use it in a brand-new scam. He'll like that."

"Mac says it's real," said Ellie.

"Mac is in league with Jackson."

"True," said Ellie. "And I haven't told him a thing. He doesn't know you contacted me or anything."

Crista was surprised. "You've talked to Mac since I left Chicago?"

Ellie hesitated. "He calls me every day. He came by last night."

"You saw Mac last night?"

"Yeah, well…" Ellie turned her head to gaze out the passenger window.

"Please tell me you didn't spend the night with Mac."

"He didn't suspect a thing. I swear. And, anyway, if I didn't let him stay over, he would have been suspicious."

"You're getting serious with Mac?"

"Not exactly serious." Still, Ellie's tone said it was more serious than she wanted to let on.

Crista smiled at the irony.

"I couldn't help myself," Ellie said. "I kept thinking it would blow over, that one of us would lose interest. And then when you and Jackson broke up—"

"We didn't *break up*. There was no relationship to start with. He was conning me. I was a mark."

"Mac thinks the world of Jackson."

"Mac is Jackson's partner. They were probably going to split the diamonds."

"You said there were no diamonds."

"Everyone seems to think there are. Otherwise…" Crista swallowed. She hated that every memory of being with Jackson made her heart hurt.

Ellie touched her shoulder.

"I'm going to get over it," said Crista. "I'm already over it. Reginald said—not that I can trust Reginald— but my new lawyer says the same thing. They said the Bahamian company is going to give me free rein on Cristal Creations. To them, it's just an investment. And they're very patient, looking for a long-term return. It's going to be great."

"I'm so glad," said Ellie.

"So am I." Crista had so much to be grateful for.

She was out from under Vern. She'd seen Jackson's true colors before it was too late. And she was about to sever the last of her ties with her father. After this, she was a free woman starting a whole new, independent life.

"That's it?" asked Ellie as a chain-link fence topped with razor wire came into view. An imposing dark gray stone building loomed up behind it.

"That's definitely it," Crista said in a hushed tone.

For the first time, she thought about what it must be like to be locked up inside the bleakness of Riverway State prison. She shuddered.

"There's a sign for visitor parking," said Ellie, pointing out the windshield. "Do you want me to come with you?"

"You can't. They needed to have your name in advance." Though the street was empty, Crista signaled right and turned into the parking lot.

She knew she needed to do this alone. Still, part of her wished she could bring Ellie along for moral support.

"It's not too late to back out," said Ellie.

Crista chose a spot and pulled in.

"This won't take long." Crista looped her purse over her shoulder, taking the manila envelope from the seat between them.

"Got a pen?" asked Ellie.

"I do."

"He's going to be surprised by this."

"He's going to be stunned by this."

Crista wasn't sure which would shock him more, that she showed up or that she was calling his bluff. In typical convoluted Trent Corday style, he'd convinced Vern that the mine was worth money. His real objective had obviously been the Gerhard wealth. He clearly thought he could get his hands on some of that if she was married to a Gerhard.

She didn't know how he'd planned to achieve that. But then, she'd never understood the conniving workings of her father's mind.

She reached for the handle and yawned open the driver's door.

"I'll be waiting," said Ellie, worry in her tone.

"I'll be right back," Crista said with determination.

She forced herself to make the long walk to the gate at the fence. There, she gave a guard her name and identification. She let him check her bag. Then a female guard patted her down before they let her in.

A pair of burly, unsmiling guards led her through a doorway and directed her down a long, dank hall. The place smelled of fish and disinfectant. Everything about it seemed hard and cold.

She was determined to feel no sympathy whatsoever for her father. He'd been guilty, no question. But on a human level, she pitied anyone stuck in here. With every step, she fought an increasing urge to turn and run.

Finally, she came to a doorway that led into a brighter room. It had high mesh-covered windows, a checkerboard floor and several small red tables with connected stools.

She scanned the room, easily spotting her father. He'd aged since she'd seen him last, his hair gray, his skin sallow and his shoulders stooped and narrower than she remembered.

When he saw her, his eyes went wide with surprise. His jaw dropped, and he gripped the table in front of him, coming slowly to his feet.

"Crista?" he mouthed.

She squared her shoulders and marched toward him.

"Crista," he repeated, and his lips curved in a smile.

She hoped he didn't reach for her. She inwardly cringed at the thought of giving him a hug.

"I need your signature," she stated up front.

"I can't believe you're here."

"I'm not staying."

"No, no." His head bobbed in a nod. "Of course you can't stay. I understand."

"I know about the mine."

He gestured for her to sit down.

She hesitated but then sat.

"I know about the mine," she repeated.

"Jackson told me."

Her chest tightened at the mention of Jackson's name. She had no intention of pursuing the discussion.

"We both know it's worthless," she said, folding back the envelope flap.

"It's not—"

"But you've obviously convinced people it has some value."

"It's not worthless."

She stared at him. "Right. You forget who I am."

"But—"

"This latest scam of yours has put me in actual danger. Vern threatened to kill me, and I think he was serious."

"He *what*?" Her father put on his shocked face.

"Please, save it."

"I never meant for—"

"Quit trying to fool me. I'm not your mark. I'm your daughter. I need one thing from you, and then I am out of your life for good."

He swallowed. He even teared up a little bit. His acting was impressive.

"What do you need?" he asked in a raspy voice.

She produced the papers. "I had a lawyer draw these up. It transfers my shares in the Borezone Mine to you."

Trent drew back.

"You and I know this is meaningless. But if there's anyone out there who believes there really are diamonds, or if you manage to convince someone in the future that there are diamonds, they'll come after you and not me. That's all I want."

His head was shaking. "It's not worthless."

"There's no point in telling me that."

He lunged for her hand, but she snapped it away.

"Check," he said. "Have a lawyer check. Better still, have a securities regulator check. At today's prices your shares are worth tens of millions."

"Ha," she scoffed, wondering why he kept up the facade.

She couldn't figure out what he hoped to gain. Then again, at the beginning of any of his cons, it was never obvious what he hoped to gain.

"Check it," he said with impressive sincerity. "Promise me you'll check it, and then you'll understand what I'm about to do."

Her suspicions rose. "What are you about to do?"

He took the papers from her hands.

"Dad?" The name was out before she could stop herself.

She saw him smile while he looked down. Was he signing?

He flipped through the three pages to the end. There, he made a stroke through his name and printed something else.

"Jackson Rush was here three days ago," he said.

"I bet he was."

Her father looked up. "He said something. Well, he said a lot of things. But he reminded me of something that I'd forgotten a long time ago."

She schooled her features, determined not to react.

"He reminded me that being your father meant something. I owe it to you to take care of you."

She wasn't buying it. "What did you just write?"

"He also showed me what he was, who he was. He's honest, principled and upstanding."

"Stop," she managed. She didn't believe a word of it, but her chest was getting tighter and tighter.

"I'm not going to accept the mine shares. But you're right. You can't keep them, either. They put you in danger. When I put them in your name, I had no idea they'd grow in value."

"They're not—"

"Stop," he said. "You're going to confirm their value beyond a shadow of a doubt. And then you're going to believe that I'll never do anything to hurt you ever again."

She didn't want to believe him. But she couldn't begin to guess his angle. If the shares weren't worth any money, she was going to find out. If they were, why wasn't he grabbing them?

"What did you write on the papers?" she asked again.

"I crossed out my own name. I replaced it with Jackson Rush's."

Her jaw dropped open, and a roar started in her ears.

"You can trust him."

She shook her head. She couldn't. She didn't dare.

"You can," her father insisted. "You know Cristal Creations is out of the Gerhard name."

How had he known that? How was it even relevant?

"Jackson did that for you," he said.

She peered at her father, trying desperately to decide if he was being honest or conning her. But she couldn't tell.

"You're smart," he said. "And you're right. Don't keep the shares. Give them to Jackson. He'll do right by you. He's the only person I'd trust."

"He'll give them back to you," she guessed. "Or he'll split them with you."

Trent smiled. "Then why don't I take them right now?"

She didn't have an answer for that.

"I conned Jackson. I used his father. I blamed the Gerhards. I told him you were in danger and counted on his principles and nothing else to get you out of it. He helped you because he's honest and trustworthy. Trust him, Crista. It's your best and only play. Don't keep these shares a minute longer than you have to."

She searched for the flaw, knowing there had to be something she didn't see. Her father would never willingly give up anything of value.

"It's exactly what it seems," he said softly. Then he tucked the papers back into the envelope. "You don't even have to believe me. You're going to verify every single thing for yourself."

Crista didn't know what to say. She didn't know what to do.

"I'll understand if you never come back," said Trent. "But I hope you will. I hope someday you'll be able to forgive me, and you'll come and see me." His eyes teared up again. "You'll come and tell me how you're doing."

Sympathy welled up inside her, and she knew she was in trouble. Despite her best efforts, he'd gotten to her all over again. She quickly scooped up the papers, jumped up and rushed for the door.

It wasn't until she was through the gate that she felt like she could take a breath. There she stopped, steadying herself.

In the distance, she saw Ellie get out of the car.

"Crista?" she called out.

"I'm coming." Crista's voice was far too dry for Ellie to hear. So she started walking. She gave a wave to show she was all right.

Ellie met her halfway. "What happened?"

"It was weird."

"Weird how? Are you okay?"

"He wouldn't sign." Crista handed Ellie the envelope.

Ellie stared down at it. "What? What do you mean he wouldn't sign?"

They came to the car.

"Take that to Jackson. Tell him to sign it and get Reginald to notarize it. I'm so done with this stupid mine."

"What do you mean, take it to Jackson?" Ellie stopped beside the passenger door, looking over the roof at Crista.

"This is going to sound crazy." It was crazy. "My father says he trusts Jackson. He doesn't want the shares for himself. He agrees I shouldn't keep them. So he wants me to give them to Jackson."

"Mac trusts Jackson," said Ellie. "And I trust Mac."

"Then we're all in agreement, aren't we?"

"Are you mad at me?"

"No."

"For saying I trust Mac?"

Crista let out a deep sigh. "I'm tired. I'm baffled, and I'm too exhausted to figure out the truth. Did you know Jackson was behind the Bahamian company that bought Cristal Creations?"

Ellie's eyes narrowed in obvious puzzlement.

"For some reason, Jackson got Cristal Creations out of Vern's hands. He's somehow set it up so that I can run my own company."

"That was an incredibly nice thing for him to do."

"I don't know why he did it."

"Why don't you ask him?"

"I can't."

"Sure you can."

But Crista knew she couldn't bring herself to face him. "If I was right about him, then I don't ever want to see him again. And if I was wrong about him, well, I doubt he ever wants to see me again."

"That's not true."

"Take him the papers. Let's get this over with."

Crista pulled open the door. By tomorrow, the next day at the latest, she'd be free of the Borezone Mine. She could finally get back to work and push Jackson out of her mind.

Jackson stared at the ownership transfer agreement for the Borezone Mine. "What's the catch?" he asked to no one in particular.

"None that I can see," said Reginald.

"Do you think her old man has really changed?" asked Mac.

"She doesn't believe they're worth anything," said Ellie.

Jackson looked up and took in the three faces. "But

they are worth something. We all know they're worth millions. I can't take them." He shoved the papers across the meeting table in his Rush Investigations office.

"That's how you protect her," said Mac.

"She definitely wants you to have them," said Ellie.

"You can still use them to her benefit," said Reginald.

"It's not the same thing," said Jackson. "They belong to her. She has every right to own them, sell them—"

"Or give them away," said Mac.

"Not to me," said Jackson.

"Then who? Give her another solution. What is she supposed to do, sit at home and wait for Gerhard to come back?"

"If only you hadn't lied to her," said Ellie.

"That's not helping," said Mac.

"She's right," said Jackson. "But I didn't think I had a choice," he told Ellie. "If I'd revealed the whole truth up front, she'd have run fast and far from me. Gerhard would have convinced her to come back."

"Maybe," Ellie allowed.

"We should have gone to Vegas," said Jackson. "It was always the best plan."

"Want me to call Tuck?" asked Mac.

Jackson coughed out a laugh. "Right. Great idea. I could kidnap her all over again."

"I wouldn't kidnap her," said Ellie.

"No kidding," said Jackson. Clearly, he had to work on his sarcastic voice.

"But you can probably persuade her."

Jackson huffed. "I can't persuade her. I wouldn't try."

He loved Crista. There was no way he'd do a single thing to cause her more hurt.

"For her own good," said Ellie.

"Not a chance."

"Refuse to sign the papers."

"I already did," said Jackson.

"Offer to marry her instead."

"I already did that, too. She turned me down flat."

"Did you tell her you love her?" asked Ellie.

"I—"

"Don't bother denying it," said Mac.

"I think she knows," said Jackson.

Everyone else had figured it out. He was starting to feel like he was wearing a neon sign. Besides, what other explanation could there be for his behavior?

"She thinks you're angry with her," said Ellie.

"Why would she think that?"

"Because she refused to trust you."

"That's just good sense," said Mac.

Jackson frowned at him.

"I'm serious," said Ellie. "She's afraid you won't forgive her."

"There's nothing to forgive." His brain latched on to the word *afraid*. Why would Crista care about his forgiveness?

Ellie gave him a secretive smile.

"Are you saying…" he asked.

"I don't know anything for sure," said Ellie.

But she suspected. It was clear Ellie suspected. She thought Crista might have feelings for him.

"Where is she?"

"She's in Wisconsin by now. But I can take you to her."

"Wisconsin?"

"Far away from Vern Gerhard."

Okay, that was good.

Mac put his phone to his ear. "I'll get Tuck to warm up the jet."

Jackson was about to protest. Tuck had already done enough. But then he calculated the time savings and decided it was worth asking. Tuck could always say no.

"Good plan," he said to Mac.

"Wisconsin only?" asked Mac. "Or all the way to Vegas?"

Jackson grinned. Persuasion and even kidnapping was starting to sound like a very good idea. "All the way to Vegas."

Crista was in her motel room staring at her email, willing a message to arrive from Ellie. Surely she'd taken the papers to Jackson by now. Surely he'd signed. Crista knew he had to be angry with her, but she also believed he'd been trying to help her. Surely he'd be willing to do this one small thing.

She hit the refresh button, but there were no new messages.

"Come on," she said out loud.

A knock on her door startled her.

Fear immediately contracted her stomach. Her first thought was that it was Vern. Had he followed her from Chicago? Had he staked out the prison? Or maybe he'd threatened Ellie and forced her to reveal Crista's location.

The knock sounded again.

Crista carefully rose to her feet. The chain was on the door, but she had no doubt Gerhard's burly security men would break it down. She could tell them Jackson already owned the shares. But she had no proof. They probably wouldn't believe her.

She started to back away, thinking she'd lock herself in the bathroom and call the police.

"Crista?" came a man's voice.

No...

"Crista, it's me, Jackson."

Relief instantly rushed from her scalp to her toes.

"Open the door," he called.

"Jackson?" She rushed forward. "Jackson?" she called louder.

"Ellie gave me the papers."

"Good. That's good." She gulped a couple of deep breaths, staring at the door.

"Ellie and Mac are in the car."

"Ellie's here?"

"Yes."

That had to be good. It was all good. Vern hadn't found her. She wasn't afraid of Jackson. He must have signed the papers. Maybe he was here to give her a copy.

Her hands trembled as she pulled off the chain. Then she turned the dead bolt and twisted the door handle, opening the door.

Jackson was there, smiling. She was glad to see him. She was ridiculously glad to see him.

"Hi," she managed.

"Hi yourself."

"Ellie brought you?" That much was obvious, but she didn't really know what else to say to him.

"Can I come in?"

"Yes." She stepped back.

She glanced out at the parking lot. "Just you?"

"I need to talk to you alone."

"Okay." She shut the door behind him.

Then she turned to where he was standing, close, looking strong and sexy and not even a little bit angry.

"You signed?" she asked, so happy to have this all behind her.

She wanted to walk into his arms. She could hug him at least, couldn't she?

"I didn't sign," he said.

She stopped herself short. "What?"

"I didn't sign," he repeated.

"Why not?"

"I don't want your diamond mine, Crista."

"But…it's just a formality. You know that. Why would you refuse?"

Had everything he'd said been a lie? Did he not care about her at all? Was he so angry he was willing to let her take her chances with Vern and Manfred?

"Is transferring the shares all about the Gerhards?" he asked.

"Yes. If I don't own the mine, they go away."

"That's true."

She was starting to get annoyed. "So? What's your problem?"

"The problem is, my earlier deal stands," he said.

"You had a deal with my father?" What secret angle had she missed? She braced herself for what he was about to reveal.

"My deal was with you."

She didn't respond. He was talking in riddles.

"Vegas," he continued. "The deal was that I'd keep you safe from Gerhard by marrying you in Vegas."

"Is that a joke?"

"But I don't think I presented it right," he said.

She was growing more confused by the minute. "It was pretty straightforward."

They got married and foiled Vern's plan.

"No." Jackson shook his head, taking a step forward

to bring them close together. "It wasn't straightforward at all. What I should have said back then was I love you, Crista Corday. Will you marry me and spend the rest of our lives together? Let's do it in Vegas, because I can't wait another second for you to be my wife."

His face went blurry in front of her and she blinked, realizing her eyes had teared up.

"What did you say?" she rasped. "You're not playing me?"

"I'm not playing you." He cradled her face with his palms. "I've never been more serious in my life."

"Because—" Her voice broke. "Because I couldn't take it if you were. Money I can lose."

"Trust in this, Crista. I love you with all my heart."

He kissed her, and joy sang through her chest. It was long minutes before he broke the kiss.

"I love you," she answered, breathless. "And I'll marry you in Vegas or anywhere else you want."

His arms went around her, and she hung on tight.

"You love me?" he asked.

"More than that. I trust you. I trust you with my heart, my soul and my life."

There was laughter in his voice. "And the diamonds, because the diamonds are very real."

"The diamonds aren't real." How many times did she have to say it?

"Maybe you'll believe it when you start turning them into jewelry designs."

"Maybe." If diamonds showed up in her workshop, she'd concede they were real.

"In the meantime, my friend Tuck is waiting at the airport with his jet."

"Oh, right. Your friend Tuck who has a jet."

"I told him he could be the best man."

"And you brought Ellie for maid of honor?"

"I brought Ellie. Though I don't know what you'll do for dresses and flowers."

"They have stores in Vegas."

"That they do. I'm sure we can find anything our hearts desire in Vegas."

She burrowed against his shoulder, drinking in the solid warmth of his body. "The only thing my heart desires is you."

He rocked her back and forth. "I am so monumentally glad to hear that."

The motel room door opened.

"Are we going to Vegas?" asked Ellie.

Crista grinned. "We're going to Vegas."

"Bachelorette at the Lion Lounge," Ellie sang.

"You'll have maybe an hour before the wedding," said Jackson. "I'd suggest you spend it shopping."

"You will need a dress." Ellie sounded disappointed.

"So will you," said Mac, his arm going around Ellie. "Something slinky. I've always had a thing for bridesmaids."

"Too much information," said Jackson.

Mac just grinned.

"I hope you have a thing for brides," Crista whispered to Jackson.

"I have a thing for one particular bride," he whispered back. "From the first second I saw her, I knew she had to be mine."

"But this time," she said, smiling up at him. "It'll be *my* dress. *My* wedding. But with you, Jackson. Forever."

* * * * *

#2461 FOR BABY'S SAKE
Billionaires and Babies • by Janice Maynard
Lila Baxter is all business. That's why she and easygoing James Kavanagh broke off their relationship. But when she unexpectedly inherits a baby, she'll have to face him again...and he might win it all this time.

#2462 AN HEIR FOR THE BILLIONAIRE
Dynasties: The Newports • by Kat Cantrell
When single mother Nora O'Malley stumbles into the reclusive life of her childhood best friend, he'll have to confront his dark past, and put love before business, if he's ever to find happiness with her little family...

#2463 PREGNANT BY THE MAVERICK MILLIONAIRE
From Mavericks to Married • by Joss Wood
When former hockey player turned team CEO finds out his fling with a determinedly single matchmaker has led to unexpected consequences, he insists he'll be part of her life from now on...for the baby's sake, of course!

#2464 CONTRACT WEDDING, EXPECTANT BRIDE
Courtesan Brides • by Yvonne Lindsay
If King Rocco does not have a bride and heir in a year's time, an ancient law will force him to relinquish all power to the enemy. Courtesan Ottavia Romolo might be the solution, but she demands his heart, too...

#2465 THE CEO DADDY NEXT DOOR
by Karen Booth
CEO and single father Marcus Chambers will only date women who would be suitable mothers for his young daughter, but when his free-spirited neighbor temporarily moves in after a fire destroys her apartment, he finds himself falling for the worst possible candidate!

#2466 WAKING UP WITH THE BOSS
by Sheri WhiteFeather
Billionaire playboy Jake expected the fling with his personal assistant, Carol, to be one and done. But when a surprise pregnancy brings them closer, will it make this all-business boss want more than the bottom line?

HDCNM0716

REQUEST YOUR FREE BOOKS!
2 FREE NOVELS PLUS 2 FREE GIFTS!

H HARLEQUIN®

Desire

ALWAYS POWERFUL, PASSIONATE AND PROVOCATIVE

YES! Please send me 2 FREE Harlequin® Desire novels and my 2 FREE gifts (gifts are worth about $10). After receiving them, if I don't wish to receive any more books, I can return the shipping statement marked "cancel." If I don't cancel, I will receive 6 brand-new novels every month and be billed just $4.55 per book in the U.S. or $5.24 per book in Canada. That's a savings of at least 13% off the cover price! It's quite a bargain! Shipping and handling is just 50¢ per book in the U.S. and 75¢ per book in Canada.* I understand that accepting the 2 free books and gifts places me under no obligation to buy anything. I can always return a shipment and cancel at any time. Even if I never buy another book, the two free books and gifts are mine to keep forever.

225/326 HDN GH2P

Name   (PLEASE PRINT)

Address   Apt. #

City   State/Prov.   Zip/Postal Code

Signature (if under 18, a parent or guardian must sign)

Mail to the **Reader Service:**
IN U.S.A.: P.O. Box 1867, Buffalo, NY 14240-1867
IN CANADA: P.O. Box 609, Fort Erie, Ontario L2A 5X3

Want to try two free books from another line?
Call 1-800-873-8635 or visit www.ReaderService.com.

* Terms and prices subject to change without notice. Prices do not include applicable taxes. Sales tax applicable in N.Y. Canadian residents will be charged applicable taxes. Offer not valid in Quebec. This offer is limited to one order per household. Not valid for current subscribers to Harlequin Desire books. All orders subject to credit approval. Credit or debit balances in a customer's account(s) may be offset by any other outstanding balance owed by or to the customer. Please allow 4 to 6 weeks for delivery. Offer available while quantities last.

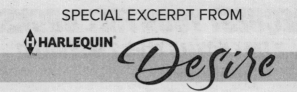
James Kavanagh liked working with his hands. Unlike his
eldest brother, Liam, who spent his days wearing an Italian
tailored suit, James was most comfortable in old jeans
and T-shirts. Truth be told, it was a good disguise. No one
expected a rich man to look like a guy who labored for a
paycheck.

That was fine with James. He didn't need people sucking
up to him because he was a Kavanagh. He wanted to be
judged on his own merits.

At the end of the day, a man was only as rich as his
reputation.

As he dipped his paintbrush into the can balanced on the
top of the ladder, he saw movement at the house next door.
Lila's house. A house he'd once known all too well.

It didn't matter. He was over her. Completely. The two of
them had been a fire that burned hot and bright, leaving only
ashes. It was for the best. Lila was too uptight, too driven,
too everything.

Still, something was going on. Lila's silver Subaru was parked in its usual spot. But it was far too early for her to be arriving home from work. He gave up the pretense of painting and watched as she got out of the car.

She was tall and curvy and had long blond curls that no amount of hair spray could tame. Lila had the body of a pinup girl and the brains of an accountant, a lethal combo. Then came his second clue that things were out of kilter. Lila was wearing jeans and a windbreaker. On a Monday.

He could have ignored all of that. Honestly, he was fine with the status quo. Lila had her job as vice president of the local bank, and James had the pleasure of dating women who were uncomplicated.

As he watched, Lila closed the driver's door and opened the door to the backseat. Leaning in, she gave him a tantalizing view of a nicely rounded ass. He'd always had a thing for butts. Lila's was first-class.

Suddenly, all thoughts of butts and sex and his long-ago love affair with his frustrating neighbor flew out the window. Because when Lila straightened, she was holding a baby.

Don't miss FOR BABY'S SAKE
by USA TODAY bestselling author Janice Maynard.
Available August 2016!

And meet all the Kavanagh brothers in the
KAVANAGHS OF SILVER GLEN *series—*
In the mountains of North Carolina, one family discovers that wealth means nothing without love.

A NOT-SO-INNOCENT SEDUCTION
BABY FOR KEEPS
CHRISTMAS IN THE BILLIONAIRE'S BED
TWINS ON THE WAY
SECOND CHANCE WITH THE BILLIONAIRE
HOW TO SLEEP WITH THE BOSS
FOR BABY'S SAKE

Whatever You're Into... Passionate Reads

Looking for more passionate reads from Harlequin®?
Fear not! Harlequin® Presents, Harlequin® Desire and
Harlequin® Blaze offer you irresistible romance stories
featuring powerful heroes.

❤HARLEQUIN *Presents.*

Do you want alpha males, decadent glamour and jet-set
lifestyles? Step into the sensational, sophisticated world of
Harlequin® Presents, where sinfully tempting heroes ignite a
fierce and wickedly irresistible passion!

❤HARLEQUIN *Desire*

Harlequin® Desire novels are powerful, passionate and
provocative contemporary romances set against a backdrop of
wealth, privilege and sweeping family saga. Alpha heroes with
a soft side meet strong-willed but vulnerable heroines amid a
dramatic world of divided loyalties, high-stakes conflict and
intense emotion.

❤HARLEQUIN *Blaze*

Harlequin® Blaze stories sizzle with strong heroines and
irresistible heroes playing the game of modern love and lust.
They're fun, sexy and always steamy.

Be sure to check out our full selection of books
within each series every month!

www.Harlequin.com

Turn your love of reading into rewards you'll love with
Harlequin My Rewards

**Join for FREE today at
www.HarlequinMyRewards.com**

Earn **FREE BOOKS** of your choice.

Experience **EXCLUSIVE OFFERS** and contests.

Enjoy **BOOK RECOMMENDATIONS**
selected just for you.

PLUS! Sign up now
and get **500** points
right away!

Earn
FREE
REWARDS
HarlequinMyRewards.com
Join
Today!

MYR16R